"WITH MONEY, YOU KNOW, EVERY-THING IS POSSIBLE."

"No, that's not true," she said.

"Everything."

"Not true."

"Everything can be bought. Everything and everybody."

"Oh," said Joan, overly casual and non-chalant. "I suppose people can be bought?"

"Of course."

"Have you bought people?"

"For business, yes."

"For love?" she asked.

He gave this some thought. "Not yet."

"So there," said Joan. "You can't buy love."

"Oh, for the right price ..."

JACK ENGELHARD

INDECENT PROPOSAL

A SIGNET BOOK

SIGNET

Published by the Penguin Group
Penguin Books Ltd, 27 Wrights Lane, London W8 5TZ, England
Penguin Books USA Inc., 375 Hudson Street, New York, New York 10014, USA
Penguin Books Australia Ltd, Ringwood, Victoria, Australia
Penguin Books Canada Ltd, 10 Alcorn Avenue, Toronto, Ontario,
Canada M4V 3B2
Penguin Books (NZ) Ltd, 182–190 Wairau Road, Auckland 10, New Zealand

Penguin Books Ltd, Registered Offices: Harmondsworth, Middlesex, England

First published in the USA by Donald I. Fine, Inc., 1988
First published in Great Britain in Signet 1993
7 9 10 8

Signet Film and TV Tie-in edition first published 1993

The author gratefully acknowledges the support of his editor, Susan Schwartz,
and his agents, Barrie Van Dyck and Blanche Schlessinger of Philadelphia

Printed in England by Clays Ltd, St Ives plc

THIS IS FOR LESLIE, DAVID AND RACHEL,
AND TO THE LOVING MEMORY OF NOAH AND IDA.

CHAPTER
1

THE MAN was playing blackjack for a hundred thousand dollars a hand. A woman sat next to him, but no one else. The table was roped off for his private use. A crowd had gathered to watch. Security officers tried to keep the people moving.

"He's losing," a day-tripper said. "He's lost ten hands in a row."

A million dollars.

Me, I'd been casing the place for a three-dollar table.

Then I'd gotten myself drawn to the crowd and then to the man. He was spectacular. In the dimness of the casino he was a vision in black. Black hair, black mustache, black suit. Tall and straight and handsome and built for a throne.

From the looks of him, he was no doubt an Arab, a prince, a member of the royal household from the depths of a desert kingdom, and worth, I figured, hundreds of millions and maybe some billions.

Royalty for sure, I thought. The man was aloof, absolute and magnificent.

"Move it, move it," the security people said.

But I was too fascinated to move, captivated as I was by this event that made time stop. This was a tribute to excess, a triumph of opulence. *So there were such people, after all.* Such people actually did play for that kind of money.

That million he had dropped, he began winning it back and then some. Even drew blackjack twice in a row.

"Good shoe," said the dealer in admiration. Only in gambling did luck count as *skill.*

The man nodded, but it was a reluctant gesture. He spoke no English, I assumed. That, or he was too exalted to accept, or even understand, praise. Nothing could touch a man like that; what could he *need?* He had enough money, obviously, to own whatever tempted him— things, for sure, and people, maybe. He had nothing in common with the rest of us except mortality, and even that was a question.

He continued to win. But win or lose, he was impervious. He had the face of a prince—masculine but also fine, sharply drawn, and washed, it seemed, by the sands of Arabia. The hands were beautiful, shaped to command by the flick of a wrist.

For me, a corporate speechwriter earning thirty-one thousand dollars a year before taxes, this performance was astonishing. All these chips being traded so nimbly and casually between man and house—any single one could have let me quit my job and join the dig for the City of David, or buy someone else a complete college education, or even a lung, a kidney, a heart . . . a *life!*

Despite this, I felt no envy, no resentment. I was too stupefied to feel anything but respect. After all, I had not been there when God gave out the money. This man had been!

But what sort of man was this, I wondered, who could so trivialize the profound, who could squander in an instant what others could not accumulate in a lifetime? Rich was one thing, but this—this was godly.

One hundred thousand dollars a hand was beyond gambling. It was more like creation, mountains and seas heaving and tossing and contesting for the exclusive right to declare sovereignty.

Who was this man?

"He's winning," a day-tripper said.

Most of the crowd watched in humbled silence, awed by this drama, mesmerized by this mighty Arab.

As for me, I was no stranger to this place and certainly no stranger to games of chance. I had seen high rollers before and big action, but nothing so lofty as this, and it deserved my attention. Would I not have paused for Beethoven in his day?

What Beethoven was to music, obviously this man was to money; and as music, literature and art spoke for the past, money spoke for the present. We wagered billions on the stock market, lotteries and casinos, and in so doing we defined our culture. Our culture was money. Millionaires and billionaires, these were our heroes.

Critical? Not me. I was here, wasn't I?

I came here often to hit the jackpot, and as yet this had not happened; but there was always this time, and next time, and meantime there was this Arab to behold.

Though I was far back, behind a wall of people, I felt something strange—a kinship with this man. Maybe it was simply a natural longing to be in there with him, in the eye of life.

Or maybe it was true that there was contact, for each time I took a step back—acting on my decision to do some gambling of my own—I noticed his head drift my way, as if to summon me hither.

You're dreaming, I said to myself. What is he to you and what are you to him? You're not even on the same planet. Oh maybe he does notice you, but as he notices the rest, as grasshoppers.

But there it was again, a movement that could not quite be called a nod—but close. Close to what? I thought. What do you want from him? You want him to anoint you? You come from your own line of kings. You are already anointed. This is not your man.

Finally, I edged clear of the crowd and began my rounds, moving and losing, from slots to roulette to craps, distracted all along by thoughts of this man. There was this about him: *possibility*. The chance for something big.

Just being near this Arab removed the curse of tedium. The trouble with life, as I had it figured, was that nothing *happened*. Every day was just another day.

But in the vicinity of this Arab, something was bound to happen. What exactly, I did not know, except that greatness produced sparks, and these could light up another man. Burn him, too, of course.

So I resisted the urge to go back, although I was tempted, and even found that I had made a circle and was now only six blackjack tables away from him.

It was a three-dollar table, so I moved in and let the lady dealer exchange forty dollars for chips. I played an uninspired game. I was doing too much thinking—like this: What does a man reach for after his first billion? Does he dream, and what can he be dreaming when he already has everything?

I remembered combat heroes from my newspaper days—a Medal of Honor recipient among them—and their sorrow when peace set in. They were not lovers of war, but they knew they'd never get to surpass or even repeat themselves. I wondered if the same applied to heroes of wealth. Such an odd despair.

"You see what's going on?" the woman next to me said to the dealer.

"He's a sheik," said the dealer.

"I thought it was Omar Sharif."

"He sure is handsome," said the dealer.

"Forget handsome. He's glorious. God!"

"Never mind glorious," said the dealer. "We're talking *rich*."

There was no escaping this man. The place was buzzing. I played a few more rounds, broke about even and then let my restless feet carry me back to this sheik.

As I made my way over I remembered this from the Midrash: A man's feet lead him to his destiny.

* * *

I was again a face in the crowd.

"Ever see gold chips?" a man said to his friend.

"Gold chips?"

"Ten-thousand-dollar chips."

"Didn't know they made them that high."

"You know it now."

I kept edging closer, and before I knew it I was up front, my knees touching the rope. These gold chips, he had them piled high, and they came and went so fast I had no idea what was going on. Was he up, down? You should not care, I told myself. *He*, I reminded myself, was not *me*.

Also, I reminded myself, he's an Arab. So he's your friend?

Back in 1967, when I was with the Fifty-fifth Paratroop Brigade, they were shooting at me from Jerusalem rooftops; and even today there wasn't much kissing and making up.

The difference here was this: This was *royalty*. Royalty was another business; and I had to admit I felt sensations. Something magical was transpiring here and I was getting hooked. I mean I started to care. I wanted him to win. I also wanted to be in there with him, only for a moment, to know what it's like in that upper world.

This was glory.

I must have been planted to the same spot for an hour. Then I thought I saw him eyeing me and I turned my face, embarrassed for me and for him. For me, especially. I felt small, here shoulder to shoulder with the mixed multitudes, the voyeurs, the scavengers.

I felt perverse taking part in this great American pastime—watching.

Enough of this, I thought. I turned to muscle through the crowd and then it happened, meaning he lifted his left arm and waved. Must be the queen of England behind me, I figured, for surely he cannot be waving at me.

"You!" he said.

"Me?"

"You."

He nodded and smiled, and kept nodding and smiling and waving me in, as you do to a reluctant pet. "Yes," he said. "You. Please. Do me the honor of being my guest. Join me."

Easy game, I thought as I stepped over the rope. Sometimes life is such an easy game.

At the same time I had an inkling about something. I don't know. Sometimes things just look too good.

Now what? So I was in this red-carpeted enclosure, where all was plush and glitter, alongside this man and this woman, and it was his move, only there was nothing coming from him. He ignored me. Was there a mistake?

For the moment I felt quite rotten and abused and even stunned inside these gates. I became conscious of my jeans, sandals, red and white polo shirt—hell, I was a regular *tourist!*

The dealer was in a tux and so were the pit bosses, about five of them, and it was all so smooth and elegant among these people, nothing at all like real life. There wasn't much talking at all here, everything was said by winks and nods, none of it my language. Food and drinks were served by the raising of a pinky finger. Even the dishes made no sounds. The hostesses moved in and out without notice.

Finally, the Arab did say something and it provoked whispering in the pit, which amounted to a riot for this respectful crew. What had he said? All I heard was this: *One.*

"Our pleasure, sir," said the dealer. "It will take a moment, sir."

With that, the dealer gathered up all the chips, counted them out and waited. We all waited.

For what I did not know.

Now he introduced himself. "Ibrahim Hassan is my name." I said my name was Joshua Kane.

He said, "Take the anchor seat, Joshua Kane."

So I did. I sat down and without staring at him I gave him the once-over. He was massive all right, meaning, by my estimation, possessed of a rare intensity. This man knew who he was. He was beyond confidence. He was power. He was all *presence.*

His woman was another story. She annoyed me. There was something askew about her. She was wrapped loosely in a dress of many colors and was darkly splendid; but unlike her man, she was not *here.*

I had seen this type in the Middle East. They were "the women." There was nothing more to be said. Ibrahim Hassan, no, I had never seen his type. They were there, I knew, out in the desert, riding the sands by camel and by jet.

"I should offer an explanation," he said.

♠ 8 ♠

"Not necessary," I said.

"You see, you have brought me luck."

I said, "You believe in luck?"

He laughed. "Luck is everything. Don't you know?"

Why yes, I thought, luck is everything. I'd known it all my life but never thought it so plainly.

"Stay awhile," he said. "I'll make it worth your time. Are you all right?"

"Yes."

"Would you care for a drink?"

"Pepsi is fine."

My answer pleased him. He was a Moslem and drinking no alcohol. Though in private, who knew?

For some reason I was scared. I had the willies. What was I supposed to be *doing*?

I forced myself to remember that once upon a time I had not been so scared of them.

Whatever we were waiting for, we still waited.

"It takes time, this," he said.

What is *this*? I thought.

"Be patient. Please."

This finally arrived—a stack of paper slips, each the shape and size of an ordinary receipt. The bundle was handed to Ibrahim Hassan and he placed a single slip on his square and then on mine, right in front of me, and written on the paper were the words *one million dollars*.

I kept cool, showing no trace of the astonishment that had me walloped.

The dealer rapidly dealt out the cards, and Ibrahim responded with the traditional blackjack signs, finger down meaning hit, palm down meaning stay. I was not impressed by his selections, especially when he split tens. This was not even basic blackjack.

But I had no say over any of this, including the cards that came to me at the anchor. I was sitting here, bringing him luck. Luck? He was getting clobbered.

Millions kept going the wrong direction. He was too damned bold.

I became protective over my square. I resented it terribly when he took the wrong action; as, for example, when the dealer's up card was six and he hit on "my" thirteen—and busted. I shook my head.

He laughed. "Play?" he said.

I shrugged.

"Go ahead," he said. "Play the anchor."

I had half expected this but it was still an intoxicating moment.

For starters, I knew I had to do something dramatic to turn things around. The first cards to arrive my way were ace and seven, meaning a soft eighteen, since the ace could count for one or eleven. The dealer's up card was eight; so, assuming he had a ten down, we'd be even, a push. A wise thing to go for.

But contrary to what I'd been bitching about, I decided to be daring and take a hit. I drew a three.

That made it twenty-one.

"Ah," said Ibrahim triumphantly.

That did it, all right. The right cards kept coming across the table and the dealer ran into a streak of bust, bust, bust. He had to hit himself—according to the rules—up to seventeen, and he kept going over twenty-one. It was beautiful. My luck was so terrific that when I drew on fourteen I'd get a seven; sixteen, I'd get a five. The ultimate sign of good luck was that I kept beating him by single points; my nineteen to his eighteen, my twenty to his nineteen.

I was motoring. I made the big money when I split eights. I drew a three on the first, a two on the second and doubled down on both, so that I had $4 million riding. I drew two picture cards to the dealer's eighteen and made myself a profit of $4 million.

Or rather, made it for Ibrahim.

Sure I lost a few hands now and then but it never got bad.

At anchor—the pivotal and most crucial spot since it was last on the players' side and thus determined the dealer's next draw to himself—I played a cunning game. I stayed on a nine (a sin) to his up three, anticipating a ten for him to bust—and he did.

I kept saving Ibrahim by these tactics, many against the book. The book wasn't here, and I was and I was hot. This was it, that sublime occasion when you can do no wrong. You ride on your self-confidence, you soar on your instincts.

I drew a murmur from the pit and a rebuke from the dealer when I called for a hit on eighteen—to his nine up card. This was absolutely never done, except perhaps by professional card-counters.

"Hit?" said the dealer.

I nodded.

Ibrahim smiled. I was his man.

The dealer announced my decision to the pit. "Player takes a card on eighteen," he said, so there'd be no doubt that it was my choice and not the house's error. He dealt me an ace and this resulted in no more than a push, but it did save the hand.

Ibrahim was amused. That smile again, so paternal. He was about my age, maybe even younger. Such perfect teeth. They seemed to go round and round and glistened as though they'd been polished and waxed. His nails obviously were. His black hair climbed up like a staircase. His eyes, he could switch them on and off and I noticed the difference. With me it was one way; with the dealer and the people in the pit he was abrupt, almost rude.

"You must lead a good life," he said.

I was surprised. He should know better than to interrupt the flow.

He had grown bored, it seemed.

It is possible, I thought, to grow bored with anything, even good things.

They say you can't be too rich or too thin. Well I don't know about thin, but rich? Maybe you can be too rich. Maybe you can even be too handsome and maybe life can be too good, so good it gets boring.

Sure enough, the tide turned.

I knew it was time to quit when I got blackjack and the dealer matched me with blackjack of his own. This was the signal that things were about to start going the other way.

Ibrahim, mediocre blackjack artist though he was, knew this, too.

♠ 12 ♠

He rose from his chair as a king rises from his throne, and this act told everybody it was over.

"Thank you," he said, and all the men in the pit nodded. A few bowed. The big boss said:

"Our pleasure, Mr. Hassan."

I wondered, can't we stay right here a while longer? We do not have to play. Just stay here, I thought, under this spell, this cloud of glory.

But it was over.

As he had ignored me there at the outset of this, so he ignored me now at the end.

What? I thought. I get nothing?

I was like the fox who lusted for the fruits in the garden. He starves himself to fit under the fence, squeezes in, has himself a feast, and then must starve himself again to get back out.

Go in empty, fill up, go out empty.

That, I'd been taught, was a parable about life—and it sure as hell was.

But I had no gripes. The money had never belonged to me—just like the fruits in the garden. I'd had my fun, even lived out a fantasy, and that was enough. Though maybe . . . maybe I had earned the right to some recompense.

Ibrahim Hassan did not think so. He had already forgotten me. But then he broke from the people who had him flanked and said, "Thank you, Joshua Kane." He shook my hand. He said, "We will do business."

Yeah sure, I thought.

CHAPTER
2

WHEN I GOT BACK to our room at the Galaxy Hotel and Casino—about five minutes down the Boardwalk from the Versailles, where I'd been with Ibrahim—it was past midnight and the TV set was on, talking to Joan as she slept. Even in slumber she was golden. She was my Main Line blonde, my high-born darling from Bryn Mawr, graduate of Shipley's and Vassar and rich places here and abroad.

All right, I thought, so you're not lucky in money. But look at this. *Look at this* . . .

If she wasn't the most beautiful woman on the planet, then who was?

More than that, she had brains and that special American kick—insolence.

What made it really good was this: She was mine!

I sometimes wondered how it had happened between us. My best guess was that we fell in love because we *didn't* understand one another, and stayed in love for the same reason—that thrill of renewal, that magic of ever-lasting discovery. In her poetic moments she said we "replenished" our lives by our conflicts. We had plenty of those.

The first came on our honeymoon when she got her period. She thought it hysterical that I refused to make love to her.

She said, "What am I—*unclean?* Josh, I keep telling you, that's so *old.*"

Maybe that was it; she was the future, I was the past. She was America, I was Europe. Forget Europe—I was Abraham setting out from Ur of the Chaldees. Yet it was that very "Hebrewness," she said, that spirit of *going forth* that drew her to me.

She said, "I think of you like that, coming out of the wilderness, in search of *something*. I think of you as that singular man, rooted to his principles, the world on one side, you on the other."

She thought I was *romantic*. French charm and all that and how, unlike other men, I looked into a woman's eyes. I was nearsighted.

She thought I had lived a life of adventure—and I had. That trek over the Pyrenees to escape Hitler. But I had been an infant through all that. I didn't know I was having an adventure.

But then I had gone off to fight for Israel in 1967, and that had been a *choice*. And there had been others. Like quitting that hot magazine job when they tried to put my byline over another man's story. She thought that showed *strength* and *character*. They hadn't thought so at the unemployment office.

In every way I numbered myself a failure, she scored me a success.

She said I was "perfect." Why argue?

She said I reminded her of that long-ago movie star John Garfield. She loved my "rugged hurt" features.

"I was sort of hoping for Cary Grant," I had told her.

"No no no. You're the outsider. The underdog. The fighter. The loner. The wanderer. You're everything I've been looking for." She said other men were so *shallow*. "A man like you comes around only once. Can't let you get away. You're Abraham, Isaac and Jacob. And David, of course. Must never forget David."

If I was Abraham, Isaac and Jacob, she was Grace Kelly, Marilyn Monroe and Lauren Bacall. Joan was more than the American dream. To an immigrant kid like me, she was America.

So I relinquished a wife and two kids for her. She gave up a husband for me, a man of wealth and social standing. Now that I had her, the job was to keep her.

In any case, you would call us a loving couple, but by no means a secure couple. No, we were afraid of each other. In return for what we had given up we demanded loyalty forever, and that was easy to promise but impossible to guarantee. Especially since our marriage was rooted in sin. She had forsaken what had been hers and I had forsaken what had been mine, and who was to say what spitefulness fate had in store?

We had even discussed it, the chance that we might each turn to another, again—and she made it a joke.

"You believe revenge bugs are flying out there?" she said.

"Yes," I said.

"Ridiculous."

Joan believed in a God of mercy. Her God knew no vengeance. If God was good—and she believed He was—then she was good. She was made in His image, after all. While we had been married to other spouses we had been adulterous, but not in her eyes. Love could not be sinful.

To Joan, the world was as pure and as bright as a kindergarten. Everything was wholesome. Everything was right. Nothing could go wrong.

Now I sat on the edge of the bed and stared abstractedly at the TV, pondering the adventure I had just had with the Arab, an episode intangible as a dream. I had nothing to show for it, no signs, no evidence to prove it, and Joan would be right to doubt that it had happened—as would I. Had it happened? Yes. What did it mean? That I did not know.

Possibly it meant that I had been put to a test and had passed. But my integrity had been stretched thin and it troubled me that I could be so easily seduced. Not that I was, but it had been close. I was vulnerable.

No doubt about it, money had become a weakness, more so with the advent of Joan. A woman like that needed things, required pampering. She deserved better, and would demand more than life on a meager income.

Besides, with or without Joan, I was tired of being poor. The big score—suddenly, that's what I was after. That's what lured me to the racetrack, to the casinos. The big score.

I had become a gambler. I lost more than I won. But I

preferred losing over stagnating, the chance of a jackpot against the certainty of need. Of course I made a salary on which we could exist. Of course we were not certifiably poor. But we were not rich, and that's poor. To me that's poor.

So I was sick of it, weary of being condemned to ordinary wages as my father and mother had been sentenced to poverty for life . . . beginning with their adventures in the New World.

For in the Old World, in France, they had been rich. And then came Hitler. They had to sell everything to pay and then bribe the smugglers who would lead them up and down the Pyrenees. By the time they reached Montreal they were penniless, especially since Father had financed the escape of twenty-two other families.

So they were destitute in Montreal and stayed destitute later in Philadelphia. "Your father, God love him, has a knack for failure," my mother once said, and since he could not succeed in business they went out borrowing.

They borrowed from friends, acquaintances, strangers and even from those families they had saved from the Roundup of Paris. Soon even those doors were shut to them. These were not happy times when they brought me along and I heard them begging for a loan—"to get us back on our feet."

The humiliation did strange things to my mother and one day she stopped talking and laughing and so she remained, hollow and impassive, until she died. That's when I promised myself, none of this for me. Not this kind of life. No no no. Never. Yet here it was, not quite but almost the same, and the fear of turning Joan into my mother obsessed me and made each moment urgent.

So I schlepped her to the casinos, and though she was a willing accomplice she rarely played and seldom joined me in the gaming rooms. And on the occasions when she did—she was so out of place!

Her beauty was of the stately kind. She was a striking paradox against the hordes of tiny women lusting after the slot machines in their orange hairdos.

This was not Joan.

She could be quite haughty and reach back into her Main Line genes for a quick score, as when she got a ticket for speeding in Collingswood, New Jersey, and tilting her head for a regal pose, she said to the officer, "You know, my father can *buy* this town."

He could, too.

Oh definitely, now and then that pride kicked up. Mostly, though, she carried herself calm and self-effacing and moderate and modest. She had once been an heiress, by golly, and a debutante, of course, and she had degrees in English and psychology, wrote poetry, read a book a week, loved art, and cried when she listened to *Concierto de Aranjuez*. The question was this: What was a girl like her doing in a place like this? She was here because her husband was here, and he was here because he had an errand—to *get rich!*

During those periods when I pursued the perfect black-jack table, as others pursued the perfect wave or the perfect sunset, she went "looking for clothes"—and given our finances that was about the extent of it; she could look but she could not buy.

"But I don't mind," she always said, "so long as we're happy and we're together." This was true as far as being together and only half true about being happy. I was not happy about being so utterly broke that Joan had to resort to the ultimate cliché: "Money isn't everything."

But it was, and this had become clear only a few days earlier, back in Philadelphia, just as we were getting into the car for this vacation, when against my advice Joan decided to check the mail.

Sure enough, there was a bill from the IRS for $1,989, remarkable for this reason: it was almost to the penny our entire savings! But—we still had money in our checking account, so the vacation was still on. Never mind that we were behind a month's rent and the landlord refused to have our front door painted—the surface peeling off as if stricken by leprosy. Such an ugly sight that, even though we resided in a relatively nice neighborhood, Joan never invited her Main Line friends to the house.

She was ashamed. She'd never admit it but she was, she was *ashamed*. Said she was too busy to have friends over anyway, for she did have a job, helping others find work, the poor and the handicapped, for which she received no salary. But she had to do it, she said, because these people *needed* her.

She was a big fan of the oppressed and the disadvantaged and agonized over the Cubans detained in American jails, apartheid, the starving children of Ethiopia, the deaf, the blind, the infirm, the aged and even Bob Brennan. Yes, Bob Brennan, the New Jersey millionaire who had been skewered on "60 Minutes" for a questionable securities business.

When they roasted him again a few months later as a summer repeat, Joan was outraged. "So unjust!" she declared, and she sent a letter off to CBS saying, "Muckraking is defendable, but not as *entertainment*."

As for our own condition, she did not see us as oppressed. Disadvantaged, maybe—but this was no big whoop. She was managing, and anyway she had faith. "Josh," she said, "I know you'll make it someday. Someday others will see in you what I see in you and on that day we'll celebrate."

Now I sat on the edge of the bed between Joan and David Letterman. He was a rerun and she was asleep and I had big news and there was nobody to hearken. I was still high over those millions—*I had played for millions*.

This had to be proclaimed. *Joshua Kane has arrived*.

I used to tell Joan the odds were turning in my favor. I was *due*. Now that it had happened the world was asleep, and so I nudged her until she wakened partly and said, "Why are you waking me? Is there a fire?"

Joan was as intense about her sleep as about her wakefulness.

"No," I said.

"So let me sleep. Good night."

"I have something to tell you," I said. "Something extraordinary happened."

But she was back to snoozing, her face dug into the pillow, her arms around the pillowcase as a drowning woman clinging to a raft, and I thought—why the rush?

I'd played for millions, yes. But not mine!

This came as a shock.

But I had been so close—so close that my life, our lives, had already taken a turn. The drought was coming to an end. I sensed *big things*. Big things were about to happen!

I got undressed, slipped under the covers and stroked her golden hair. It took me hours to fall asleep, thinking, *Nothing bad must ever happen to this woman. She is mine to safeguard, and I will. I will. I will show her. I will show them all. Only the best for her. Only the best.*

CHAPTER
3

THE NEXT MORNING we were in the shower together and I had already dropped the soap so she would get down and just then I heard the phone ring and she said never mind the phone, but I dashed out naked and dripping, slipping on the tile, and when I got to it the ringing was over and I'd never know who it was. Or maybe I would.

I dialed the operator and she said, yes, there was a message, from Ibrahim Hassan, and he'd be calling later. I felt something between dread and ecstasy.

"Of course I believe you," she now said, and it was obvious that she did but with reservations, meaning that she did not take it seriously, this great event of last night She was in one of those sassy moods.

We were having breakfast in the Galaxy Coffee Shoppe, and though it was late morning, we had got ourselves a prize booth facing the ocean and the Boardwalk.

As we gazed out the big windows, the sun was beginning to burn through the clouds, haze still covered the waters and the overnight wind had calmed to a hot breeze. The joggers and bikers appeared and disappeared as if staged, and we were the spectators enjoying the show. We were happy. Happy that it was summer and that we were here at the shore, in Atlantic City, with the sun and the sea, and the gambling so that anything might happen—and last night it almost had. If only I could convey it to Joan. The college boys from England were pushing their white two-seat rolling chairs, seeking passengers, and now the tram, half filled, slowly passed by.

Joan was wearing something loose and pink, bringing out the flush of her face, so fresh, smooth and clear. Her eyes were lit. She was incredibly beautiful. I tried to imagine her old, and could not. Impossible. I banished an image that had deceitfully invaded my mind: Joan dead.

Never! Some people should never die. It wouldn't be fair.

I told her Ibrahim Hassan had called, at least I got a message from him, and that he'd be calling back. She said, "Is this the same Abraham you've been telling me about?"

"How many Abrahams do we know?" I said. "And his name is not Abraham, it's Ibrahim."

"Oh. Forgive me."

"You're being so smart this morning."

"I simply don't understand the fuss, my darling Josh."

"Guess you had to be there," I said.

"What does he want?"

"Want? What does he want?"

"Well, you said he's calling you back. Yes, what does he want?"

"Beats me."

"Well he wants something."

"Come on, Joan."

"Where's your cynicism?" she asked.

"I don't bring it to Atlantic City."

"He wants something," she said.

"I have nothing to give."

"We all have something to give."

Strange for her to be so cautious. More like her to be first in her sorority to date a black man (and retain her chastity until she got married), and race thoroughbreds in Virginia, and surf the waves of California and even, once, ride the back seat of a Hell's Angels motorcycle. *That* was Joan.

I said, "I brought Ibrahim luck last night. Maybe that's what I have to give."

"You say he's a billionaire, this Abraham . . ."

"Ibrahim, Joan."

"This Ibrahim. You say he's a billionaire—and *he* needs your luck?"

"Maybe I need his."

"Aha! Now we're talking. You want something from him. Admit it, Josh, you do."

"I do not."

"You do, too." She shook her head and then posted loving eyes. "Sometimes, Josh, you're so transparent. You can be such a boy. Men never do grow up. But then, that's what charms the daylights out of us poor helpless women."

"Joan, my life changed last night. That's all."

"Oh?" she said, flashing that brilliant smile. "But you look the same."

There, I thought, she's into that Main Line tease, devilishly irreverent and playful, making herself a bad girl for the delight of it, savoring the exasperation she provoked.

There was also this—her fear of losing her individuality inside the man she loved. So to defend her uniqueness she rebelled, and not only against me but against anything that suggested authority. There was a story, which she never denied, that when her English professor declared Kafka an overrated talent she—this daughter of Old Money and Protestant ethics—gave him the finger.

"So do we forget the beach this afternoon?" she said.

"Why?"

"I thought we'd stay in our room and wait for Abraham to phone."

"Not funny, Joan. But yes, I am waiting for his phone call."

"But you don't know why."

"No, I don't know why."

"But you are expecting something exciting. Like maybe he'll crown you prince."

"In a sense he already has. Like the man who shook the hand of J. P. Morgan on the floor of the New York Stock Exchange. He said, 'Mr. Morgan, I would like you to do me a favor.' Morgan said, 'I have already done it, sir.' All right? So that's what Ibrahim did. Joan, read my lips. I played for *millions!*"

"But his," she said. "Not yours."

"Good guess "

"Are you really that impressed by money? You shouldn't be. It's unbecoming."

Her remark embarrassed me and I asked for the check. The Galaxy restaurant was getting crowded anyhow, though these were my people. My fellow Americans and my fellow gamblers, here for the cure as I was. As if in Lourdes, here we were, the financially lame. Here to make the correction. There had been a mistake. We hadn't received it at birth, we had failed to earn it by the work of our hands, so we were here to wrest it from Lady Chance. Heaven had forgotten to bless us. Maybe a slot machine or blackjack table would hear our prayer.

Even the rich were here for the same reason. Is anybody rich enough?

We went for a stroll on the Boardwalk as was our custom after breakfast, and it was true that I resisted each step that took me from the Galaxy and Ibrahim's phone call. What did he want? Was it something good or something bad? Or nothing at all?

"Maybe he won't even call again," Joan said, "and you'll have to go back to life as a commoner."

I didn't mind the ribbing but wasn't nuts about what she had said before, about it being unbecoming, my being so impressed by money. For money, her mother the Main Line matriarch had tried to split us up. Out there in Bryn Mawr, visiting her parents for Christmas, her mother had hustled me aside, saying, "My daughter plays tennis and golf. What do you play?"

Play, I thought. Does everyone have to *play*?

"She rides horses."

"I once rode a horse," I said. "His name was Malcolm."

"Do you belong to things?"

"Nothing at all," I had said.

"I mean clubs and fraternities and chambers of commerce and the like. Joan belongs to everything."

"Everything?" I said.

"Everything," she said.

"I guess that's possible. Maybe not desirable."

"What's your passion?"

Did I dare say Israel on the Main Line? Was it polite? I did and she said, "That's a country."

"I know."

"Have you ever been to Europe?"

"I *come* from Europe."

She said, "This won't last, you know. This marriage. Joan has rich tastes."

"I know it won't last," I said.

"You know?"

"We thought we'd give it a try for a year or two."

"That's not funny."

Her father, he was funny. He told this joke about Jesus, the four ways we know he was Jewish: "He didn't leave home till he was thirty. He went into his father's business. His mother thought he was God. He thought his mother was a virgin."

"Father!" Joan had said. "That's positively offensive."

To which her father responded, "Babe, nothing is offensive."

Later I had said, "Father? You call your father Father? Not Dad or Daddy?"

"I love him," she said, "but we're not alike. Frankly, I can't believe they're my parents. In fact I don't."

By this time she had already been disinherited on my account. How much, I asked, was he worth?

"No more, no less than any other flesh."

"You know what I mean."

"Oh what's the difference, Josh? You and money."

"I want to know. It's titillating."

"Ten million. So I hear."

"Dollars?"

"It's all tied up."

"But you gave that up for me? You're crazy."

"I have no idea how much of that was to be mine. And I don't care. Anyway, it would be more like several hundred thousand, so don't get too high on yourself. Besides, he'd have to die first and he never will."

Joan never defended her father and only once her mother. A high school principal had complained that Joan was sensitive and her mother had replied, "Exactly, sir. Joan was *raised* to be sensitive."

Joan liked that and so did I.

I never told Joan about my conversation with her mother. I also never told her mother that I played hockey and baseball because hockey was not the same as tennis and baseball was not the same as golf. I also never told her that forget horses, I rode camels in Sinai and tanks in Golan.

When we got to Ocean One, Joan sensed the urgency of my mood and we turned back and she said, "Still thinking big thoughts?"

"Listen," I said, "before this year is out I'm buying you a mink coat. I'm buying us a house. I'm buying you a car. Yes, a car. I'm bound to get hot. I told you, I'm due."

The car, our one and only car, was a Malibu that had just turned thirteen. This machine had a terrible problem—in human terms, flatulence.

The backfiring from the tailpipe was constant, and as loud as machine-gun blasts. The loudest "Bang!" came right after the engine was turned off. Windows shook. People dove for cover.

But as we got close to the Galaxy it was she who brought up Ibrahim, and she did not call him Abraham.

"You say he's handsome," she said.

"Oh yes—and there was something else about last night. I proved something."

"Oh?"

"That I'm not a slave to people like that."

"Oh?"

"Cut it, Joan."

"All right. How are you not a slave to people like that?"

"I won all this money for him and he promised to make it worth my time."

"Maybe slip you a couple of million."

"You're not being serious, Joan."

"He didn't keep his word, right? Just like an Arab."

"Joan, you're being very bad."

"Well isn't that the point?"

"No!"

"You don't hate Arabs."

"I don't hate anybody."

"Even Arabs."

"That's another story and we're not talking about that."

"That's right. We're talking about Ibrahim."

I said, "He's so rich he's not even an Arab anymore."

She laughed. "So this Arab who isn't even an Arab he's so rich . . ."

"He owns people, Joan."

"Nobody *owns* people, Josh."

"Oh, he does. But last night he didn't own me."

"How so?"

"I didn't ask for the money. It was coming to me but I did not get up on my hind legs begging."

"Yes, I know," she said, "like your parents. You're very sensitive about that still and won't take a penny that's not yours—but this wasn't borrowing, Josh. I'm sorry. You should have been paid."

"What about self-esteem?"

"If you had self-esteem, Josh, you would have demanded what's yours."

"No."

"Yes. He took advantage of you and I don't like that. Don't they do enough of that where you work?"

"I get paid."

"They take advantage of you, Josh. So did Ibrahim. But you know what I think? I think that's why he's calling you. I think he's calling you to pay you for all you did last night. It's only right."

I agreed. He owed me and it was time to pay up.

By the time we got back to our room at the hotel we were very satisfied with ourselves for having arrived at this satisfactory conclusion. When we walked in, sure enough there was the red message light blinking on the phone.

"Don't call yet," said Joan. As she slipped out of her clothes I agreed it was unseemly on my part to be overly anxious about Ibrahim. Joan and I made love, even tried something new, and when came the big bang she yelped the big yelp followed by sighs and whimperings, and this, I thought, the sounds—this was more special than anything.

Not like people married for almost three years, we still made love like people in danger. Like infidels.

Then I dialed the operator and she gave me the information.

"Ibrahim," I said. "Left his number. Wants me to call him."

"Well?"

"I don't know."

"But you were so eager. As if your whole life depended on this."

"Now I'm thinking."

I wasn't sure. I was troubled. I had not told the man where I was staying yet he knew where to reach me. A man like that, of course, had ways. That was not what troubled me.

An ordinary friendship was out of the question. I was not in his league. Not even in the minors. He wanted something from me all right. Even at the blackjack table, enthralled as he was in our game, I felt the press of his attention. He *knew me*.

Even when I had been a face in the crowd I sensed his pull. He had me singled out. When he beckoned me to join him, the gesture, the raising of the royal hand, the turn of the regal face, was no impulse. He had it planned. The more I thought of it the more certain I was that I was being set up.

For what?

That was a joke, of course—that I brought him good luck. He wanted something else.

"I'm ready for a night out on the town with the world's richest man," said Joan. "How about you?"

Joan was ready for anything, always. She lived by the philosophy that everything ought to be tried *once*. She did not believe in a hereafter. This life was the beginning and the end.

I dialed Ibrahim's number at the Versailles, the number to his suite, and there was no answer. I let the phone ring seven times before I hung up. Joan was disappointed—but then the phone rang.

"This is Joshua?"

"Yes."

"Thank you for returning my call," said Ibrahim.

I asked him how he knew I had called. He knew more than that.

"You rang seven times," he said.

Which told him something; that I was interested. A man did not let a phone ring seven times unless he was interested, and Ibrahim had been there, at the other end, counting, measuring the degree of my vulnerability.

"We ended it too quickly last night," he said. "I never

♠ 35 ♠

had a chance to repay your kindness. The rudeness was completely mine. You were extraordinary, Mr. Kane. I must make amends. Would you and your wife join us for dinner tonight?"

How did he know I had a wife? My wedding ring, to be sure.

"We already have plans for dinner," I said to win back the advantage of indifference.

"That's a shame," he said.

"Thank you for calling," I said.

"Tomorrow night then. Yes, we'll have dinner tomorrow night. I insist."

We made arrangements and after I hung up, I said, "The prince insists."

Joan was thrilled. She did a pirouette. Then she hugged me—or was it someone else?

CHAPTER
4

WE GOT to the beach early the following day because Joan said she wanted a quick start on the sun—she was still "too white" in places. A jealous person might wonder about her resolve. We were meeting Ibrahim this evening. Fortunately I was not a jealous person and didn't ask why this lady, usually so casual about her abundant good looks, suddenly required embellishments.

She was stretched flat on the blanket like a corpse, facing up, eyes firmly shut, silent for now. I knew she was alive because when the sun moved so did she, afraid to be cheated out of a single ray.

Around us were other bodies, scattered left and right as far as the eye could see, some under white and red beach umbrellas. Everyone was relaxed and slow, into a beach tempo, and the sounds of talk and laughter and radios were soft, muffled by the waves that came in sparkling off the horizon.

I heard that familiar drone and looked up. A plane

bearing an advertisement for a seafood restaurant passed
overhead. Down by the water couples were walking hand-
in-hand, the young tossing Frisbees, the even younger
building sand castles. To me the beach was a good time—
only hurry up and get it over with.

Joan had brought the Walkman along and we were
listening to Má Vlast—she had a knack for finding the
right station amid the swarm of hard rock—and I wondered what she was thinking.

In college, at NYU, I wrote a short story about a man
who arrives home unexpectedly. He is happily married
and his wife is utterly loving and devoted to him and no,
he does not catch her in bed with another man. But this:
he hears her talking on the phone and saying, "Oh he's
such an asshole."

He turns and never comes back home, devastated to the
end of his days.

I had based the story on an actual person, and though
the story never got published it was a thought that always
intrigued me—that we never know what another person
is thinking. We don't know the human heart. Not even
our own.

So it was Má Vlast on the radio and it was goosebump
time when it came to the Moldau, which Smetana had
written for a Czech river and which Israel had taken for
its national hymn, "Hatikvah." When this refrain began
to swell Joan turned for an instant to smile and pat my
face. "That's you," she whispered. "My hero."

She understood this and then again she didn't. She
certainly didn't that time she had said she wondered, only

wondered, if it was worth having a country if it meant killing innocent people. Meaning, I supposed, the Arabs, two hundred million of them, all innocent, against three and a half million Jews, all guilty, as usual.

But she was mostly a pacifist and had meant no harm, though I had a bad habit of getting emotional about all this. My father was partly to blame.

It began in May 1948, in Montreal. We were still fresh and raw from escaping Hitler and losing the rest of the family. My father had walked up Fairmount Street to buy the Yiddish paper and came back in tears, not for the headline that declared Israel a state, but for the glorious picture on the front page. He said, "Look. A Jewish soldier!"

So that's what I became in 1967; not a hero, but a Jewish soldier. I got on a plane and met a man named Dovid ben Yiddidya, who said, "We're looking for a pitcher."

I said, "Softball or hardball?"

He said, "Grenades."

I became a pitcher for Zahal, the Israel Defense Forces—nobody there knew how to throw, not like an American—and they gave me a uniform and said follow those men.

I got to know Shmuel and Shlomo, Moshe and Doodoo, Gavie and Hezie, Avi and Avri, Yonah and Yanni. There we were in Sinai and I pitched against Egypt. When Sinai was taken we roared back and I pitched against Jordan, and we won, and I knew we won when we stood by the Western Wall and I heard the shofar and everybody wept.

This nobody would ever understand.

Now I was getting tired of the beach and anxious about our upcoming evening with Ibrahim. Then, the urge hit me—the urge to gamble. Maybe now it would happen, the million-dollar hot streak, and there'd never again be a need to suck up to anybody.

"I'm going back to play some," I said to Joan. "You coming?"

She was surprised.

"Restless?"

"I guess."

"You're a bad boy."

"I know."

"I'm staying. Meet you back here."

Women—women like Joan—did not understand the *urge*. Why just beyond this beach was the real action, the casino. Blackjack tables, row after row, *waiting*.

What a waste, what a crime, what a sin to detain these green-felted high places of destiny. *Money was waiting to be won.* Suppose—and here the urge reached fever dimensions—suppose you were fated for an incredible run but weren't there! You were on the beach.

So I went and I played for about fifteen minutes. That was all I needed to be up sixty-five dollars.

But then I played for five more minutes.

CHAPTER
5

JOAN WAS WHERE I had left her.

"Back so soon?"

"I didn't want to win too much. I'm setting them up."

"Huh!" she laughed.

"Remember that time I won three hundred dollars? What happened to those days?"

"Maybe it's time for a new hobby," she said.

"Like stamp collecting," I agreed.

"Has it occurred to you that you may never get rich at the casinos?"

"No, it hasn't."

"They're not here to make you rich, Josh. They're in business to make themselves rich."

"So how are we supposed to make it, Joan, if not by my gambling? Certainly not by my working."

"You'll make it, Josh. I know you will. You'll make it on your talent."

"My talent is gambling."

"Oh."

Now I sat down beside her and we were silent for a while. Then I said, "Haven't you had enough sun?"

"I feel so good," she said. "I wish we could stay here all summer."

We were lucky to have a week—and in less than three days even that would be over and back in Philadelphia we'd resume real life. The Galaxy's public relations man, Sy Rodrigo, was a friend from my newspapering days and he had gotten us the room here for half price.

"You're tanned enough."

"Soon."

"I don't like my women well done."

"Like them rare, huh?"

"Tender."

She was listening to the waves or whatever it is women listen to when they crawl into themselves.

"I never want to die," she said.

"I've thought about that," I said.

Her eyes were suddenly red and puffy.

"Hard to imagine," she said. "I mean all these people on the beach, one day they'll all be dead. Even the kids."

"Wow. Are you that unhappy?"

"No, I'm happy. That's why I'm so sad."

"You're happy."

"Very happy. Really, I am."

Why, I wondered, is she happy?

I said, "He's a handsome guy, this guy."

"I'm sure he is."

"To tell you the truth, I could be jealous."

"I'm always jealous."

"About me?"

"I see how they look at you."

"I don't."

"I do."

"You should see how they look at him. That lady next to me, before I went over, she kept saying how handsome and glorious he was. She was having multiple orgasms out there on the casino floor."

"Ha!" she laughed, her voice rising and hitting that note of delight that was patently hers.

"I'm not kidding."

She was face up, eyelids set tight against the sun.

"I think jealousy is good," she said.

"You think everything is good."

"You're only happy when you're sad."

"Then I know where things are coming from."

She turned over. "Rub my back."

I did and my bathing trunks started getting too tight.

"Stop it," she said.

"Stop what?"

"You know what. You're bad. You're such a bad boy. What was it like?"

"Where?"

"When you were in the desert. Is this what you dreamed about? Is this what men dream about?"

"Yes."

"Did you kill anybody? You'll never tell me, will you?"

"Certain things a man never tells a woman."

"Certain things a woman never tells a man."

"Like what?" I asked.

"Uh-uh. You first."

"If I tell, you'll tell?"

"Maybe. Is it true men get erections when they're in combat?"

"What kind of Main Line crap is that?"

"It's what they say."

"Bullshit."

"All right. Well I'm not telling."

"Telling what?"

"My secrets. Guess I'll take my secrets to the grave."

"Main Line women don't go to a grave. They go to a party."

"You don't know a thing about Main Line women."

"Never will, either."

"Shut up and keep rubbing."

"Your turn."

"Later."

"Aha."

"Filthy mind."

"Why is it good?"

"What?"

"Jealousy."

"Because."

"A woman of mystery," I said. "That's you."

"I'm glad you're a war hero."

"I thought you hated war."

"I do. But I like heroes. I feel you can protect me from anything."

"I don't know about *anything*, Joan."

"I'll deny I ever said it, but a woman likes to feel protected by a man."

"This could cost you your membership."

"Tell me what a man wants "

"I don't know."

"You don't know?"

"I don't know. It's not simple."

"Well, for example, what do you want from me?"

"Everything, I guess."

"Everything? That's what men want from women?"

"I don't know."

"You're a big help."

"I never do well in surveys."

"Let's never be jealous."

"I'm game."

She turned up.

"Let's always be happy," she declared.

"It's up for grabs?"

"Yes."

"I'm not so sure."

"You just decide, that's all."

"Really."

"People make that choice," she said, "right at the beginning of their lives. They make the choice."

"Sometimes the choice makes them. Things happen."

"Not if you don't want them to."

"Joan."

"It's a choice."

"All right."

"When you get up in the morning you decide to be happy or sad. Everybody does that, consciously or not."

"Suppose you decide to be happy but they're waiting for you?" I said.

"Who?"

"I guess you wouldn't know."

"You would."

"Not even talking about myself."

"Sounds so ominous. They're waiting for you!"

"That's what I mean."

"Well I don't know what you're talking about."

"Yes you do."

"All right, let's just say I don't want to know. Not today. I've decided to be happy."

She rolled over and showed that lovely Main Line posterior. In their bikinis women are so simplified, one of this, one of that, two of those, and sometimes you wonder what all the commotion is about. I gave her tush a light spank.

"We never tried that," she said. "I mean S and M."

"How do you know about S and M?"

"Oh, I read."

"Where did you read about S and M?"

"The Bible. Why are religious people no better than others?"

"They're usually worse."

"I know," she said. "Strange. They should be better."

"People are people."

"You'd think they'd be better, knowing all those commandments. Remember that rabbi?"

"Remember that priest?"

"He wasn't a priest," she said.

"All right."

"He wasn't Catholic."

"Fine."

"It's not all the same. You think it's all the same. Talk about naive."

"He was a man of the cloth, man of the Bible."

"I don't think we need the Bible," she said.

"There'd be chaos."

"People would know the rules."

"Even with the rules people don't know the rules. Look what's going on."

"What's going on?" she said.

"Joan."

"All right, I know what's going on. I don't want to know what's going on."

"Good for you."

"We've been through this before," she said. "This isn't beach talk. Good night."

I stretched out on the towel and shut my eyes and tried to do what people did.

"I can never sleep on the beach," I said.

"Relax."

"That's the point. I can't relax."

"Hmmm," she cooed. "This is heaven."

"Ninety degrees is closer to that other place. How can you sleep under this sun?"

"I can't. Not with you yapping."

"Time to go in," I said.

"No. I know what you're thinking."

Wasn't that exactly how it had all begun?

When we first met she was the lone female among twenty of us gathered on the fifty-sixth floor of the Empire State Building for a meeting on business ethics sponsored by my company.

She was very beautiful and very professional. She wore a blue business suit that concealed everything but her tapered American legs, and when I thought of her legs, as we sat around a big table talking ethics, she pushed the hem of her skirt over her knees. I knew we were communicating, not necessarily about ethics.

"I know what you're thinking," she said during the coffee break.

Alarmed, I said, "What?"

"It's all a joke to you."

"And you? Are we really talking ethics or how to put it over?"

"I think these people are sincere, yes," she said.

"I'm not so sure they're even people. They're corpies."

"Corpies," she said. "Your word?"

"Yes."

"And corporate people aren't people."

"They're corporate people. Corpies."

"And what are you?" she asked.

"I'm a corpie, too."

"Am I a corpie?"

"Look at you," I said. "Business suit. Even a tie. Briefcase instead of a purse. That tight smile."

But it really wasn't tight at all, that smile. Instead it was like something blossoming.

"Go ahead," she said. "Tell me more."

Wait a minute, I thought. This is flirting.

"You're a corpie," I said. "At least on the outside."

"Oh," she whispered, "you know what's inside?"

"I see right through you, too."

"Huh!" She brushed by, shoulders rising and expanding. I liked those wide shoulders, so typical of the rich and the spoiled. I measured the lady as strong-willed, quick-minded, sort of happily married. Missing something, though. There was something missing in her life. The laugh was the giveaway. There was a cry in it.

When the meeting was over everybody shook hands and said, "Good meeting." I met her at the elevator—we just happened to be there together after everybody else had gone—and she said, "Good meeting." I said, "Never say good meeting."

"Why not?"

"It's so eighties."

"So corpie, would you say?"

"Men and women used to ask each other different questions."

"Oh. Like what?"

"Did you come?"

"You mean sexually."

"Now they say, did you have a good meeting?"

"Not sexually. I see. Well that's your problem."

"Problem?"

"Women mean sex to you. Yes, that's a problem. Where have you been?"

"In all the wrong places, that's for sure."

"You're a very old-fashioned person," she said. "I'm not saying that's bad. I'm not saying it's good, either. But it is you."

"And you see right through me," I said.

"I'm beginning to."

"Good or bad?"

"I just told you. I don't know. But interesting."

"Did you have a good meeting?"

"Yes," she laughed. "Did you?"

"Would you care to take a ride to the top? I understand on a clear day you can see Camden, New Jersey."

We saw New York too and it was windy up there atop the Empire State Building. She used four fingers to brush the hair off my forehead and finally asked me about the cane I'd been carrying.

"Left knee," I said. "The war, you know."

"Can't they operate?"

"Don't want them to. Only acts up once a year for a couple of weeks."

"I'd get it fixed."

I had to explain that there always had to be something wrong with you and if you fixed what was wrong something else was sure to go wrong that was even worse.

"Superstitious!" she said. "Good God!"

"I am not superstitious. It's bad luck."

She said, "I admit there's something about it, that cane. Romantic? It did help me notice you."

"I needed no such help."

We took a cab to Greenwich Village and I showed her Bleecker Street and recreated it for her as it had been in the sixties. I showed her the Bitter End where I had been a doorman and where at night a generation came to life. I mentioned the names Lenny Bruce, Bob Dylan, Peter, Paul and Mary.

We walked up to the front of the place and she said, "It's a bar now."

"Yes," I said.

She said, "Let's go back uptown. Let's go to the Algonquin Hotel for something to eat. I've always wanted to pretend I'm Dorothy Parker. People were so smart and witty then."

We agreed that some people, maybe most, whether through reincarnation or not, yearned to be cast in another generation. "You definitely are not eighties," she said. "Let's see. I'd say you belong . . ."

"I go back to the time of King David."

"I thought so. He's your hero."

"Lover, poet, warrior, sinner, king, yes, he's my man."

"Which of those are you?" she asked.

"One—but I don't know which one."

She laughed. "I'll take the poet."

I said, "What makes him my hero, above everything else, is that tremendous faith he had. I have my moments but can't seem to master that, this powerful faith. That, plus—he was so vulnerable. His great frustration was that God wouldn't talk to him, as He had talked to the prophets beginning with Abraham. So, instead, he talked to God. That's how we got the Psalms."

"You actually read the Psalms?" she said.

"What else is there to read?"

"*The Catcher in the Rye.*"

"Your book?"

"Yes," she said. "I wrote that book."

"Does J. D. Salinger know this?"

"That's the secret. Everybody who reads it thinks she wrote the book."

"I guess I get that feeling sometimes when I hear Beethoven. You become Beethoven. She, did you say?"

"Don't be like that," she said.

"But Holden Caulfield is a boy."

"He's whatever you want him to be. To me he's a girl."

We discussed other great books and the duds they may have been had the titles been rearranged. I offered *Peace and War* but she triumphed with *The Karamasov Brothers.*

"Maybe you're not such a corpie after all," I said.

She squeezed my hand and said, "Joshua, I'm a happily married woman. I've only had one affair and that was ages ago. I was getting even with my husband for a night he admitted he had with a whore out of town. We weren't getting along. We're getting along fine now and I don't need anything else. I mean things are fine the way they are. I'm a very busy person and don't have time for getting involved. I like you. You're nice. You're different. You're provocative. You're refreshing. But . . ."

I said nothing, watching Manhattan instead.

"Yes," she said, "I'm attracted to you. I think you know that. We both know something happened. We're not children. But it's all chemistry, nothing but chemistry, and I'll be over it an hour after we go our separate ways. I've been tempted before and I'll be tempted again. That's life. But nothing will happen. I've made the decision."

I wasn't sure, but she seemed to be sobbing. Her eyes got swelled up.

"I cry easily," she said. Then she said, "That's not true. I haven't cried in years."

"Sorry if I make you unhappy."

She smacked my face gently. "Don't be so arrogant."

"Arrogant?"

"Yes, arrogant. You know it's the opposite. There is a feeling . . . and I do love the feeling."

"But it's all chemistry," I said.

"Molecules and stuff."

"Nothing will happen."

"Nothing," she said. "That's a guarantee."

"Money back."

"Money back."

"What about my feelings?"

"You have no feelings. You're a man."

"Good point."

"All right. Are you saying you're attracted to me? I mean in a very special way?"

"Well I've got this feeling that says I need you."

"Oh never never need me. Bad word."

I said, "Don't you ever need anyone?"

"Never."

She leaned over and kissed my cheek.

"Is that a Main Line kiss?" I said.

"How did you know I was from the Main Line?"

"I just told you. That kiss."

"It says Main Line?"

"Oh sure. So gentile."

"How do they kiss where you come from?"

"I come from France," I said, and I showed her.

Then she said, "How did I do?"

"Still Main Line. Needs work," I sighed. "But of course you've already decided."

"That's right, I've made the decision." Why did I think otherwise? "Don't look at me like that."

Actually, I had been staring at her teeth. She could do commercials for toothpaste. Her hair, she could do commercials for shampoos. Her skin, Noxzema should pay her a fortune for a testimonial. Her upper lip, however, on the left side, was slightly but noticeably puffy. That gave her that occasional lisp.

"Benign tumor," she said.

"Where?"

"The lip. They found a tumor but it was benign. I had it fixed and nothing else went wrong."

"And I thought you were the perfect . . ."

"Shiksa?"

"Now why would you say a thing like that?"

"Because it's one reason we're so attracted to each other. We're so different and it's exciting, the unknown. You're King David and I'm Dorothy Parker."

"Maybe Bathsheba," I said.

"Is shiksa a bad word?"

"Depends how it's used."

"If we had met first, I probably would have become your shiksa."

"You like that word."

"Shiksa? Yes. I like Jewish words. Like shmatteh and schmuck. You're a shmatteh."

"That means rag."

"It does? What does schmuck mean?"

"Am I a schmuck?"

"Yes, you're a schmuck. I'm a shiksa and you're a schmuck."

"Am I a big schmuck?"

"Yes, you're a big schmuck."

"Schmuck means prick."

"It does not."

"Does so."

"You're awful. The way you lured me in! That's terrible. I have one word for you."

"What?"

"Schmuck."

The dining room of the Algonquin was empty, this late in the afternoon, but all the tables were ready, decked out in white linen. We were seated by a hauteur waiter and ordered a round of apple pie and coffee.

"Where is everybody?" she said.

"No Dorothy Parker. No George S. Kaufman. What a disappointment."

She complained that the pie was cold. She seemed to have run out of good humor. "I think we should take the next train back to Philadelphia," she said. "I'm ready to go home."

"Getting ready for that hour?"

"What hour?"

"You said an hour after we go our separate ways you'd forget about me."

"Did I say that?"

"Yes."

"I don't remember saying that. All right, maybe it will take two hours."

Then the bill came. An enormous amount.

"We should have gotten an estimate first," I said.

"Just for pie and coffee?" she said. "I can't believe the bill."

I said, "For this kind of money they should throw in a room."

She said, "All right. Let's."

We astonished each other many different ways in that room in the Algonquin, but the highlight—perhaps the greatest moment in the history of mankind—was the beginning, when she stood there, boldly upright, so firm and so soft, so blonde and so white, and staring me in the face, she stepped out of her pink panties.

"I thought you couldn't sleep here," she now said on the beach in Atlantic City.

"I wasn't sleeping."

"What were you thinking about?"

"Nothing."

CHAPTER
6

JOAN WAS GETTING spiffed up in a shapely all-white evening dress. Dinner was at six and it was late. She seldom spent much time fussing about herself, it was all there to begin with, but today was special. She had discovered a wrinkle under her right eye, nothing there really but she kept staring at it until I told her the flaw was in the mirror, not her face.

She chuckled and said, "You don't know how right you are. Some mirrors are so unflattering." She was putting on lipstick and said, "Some mirrors make you look so good. Like our mirror at home. This one's exacting and cruel. I'm getting old, Josh."

"Fortunately you're not the only one."

For some reason she stepped up and kissed me. She smelled nice and fresh and young. She was in high spirits.

Just as I was tying my tie she said, "You're wearing *that?*"

"Why do women always wait until you're dressed before telling you what you *shouldn't* wear?"

"Because we're bad. We're all bad. We do everything we can to make life miserable for you guys. Don't you know that?"

"Of course I know that."

"Now take off that tie and take off that shirt. Here."

So I changed because in this department she was the boss and she said, "That's more like it. Now you're handsome. Guess I never told you I married you strictly for your looks. I took one look at you and I said, that's *him*."

"Aha."

"I did. Isn't it funny? I mean attraction. We don't really know what it is. It's such a mystery what makes two people fall in love—nothing to do with logic or reason."

"You once said it's all chemistry."

"Well it is," she said as she hooked on the necklace with the diamond drop and measured the distance between that and her cleavage, if it could be called that. She wasn't large there, only perfect, her breasts the perfect size for loving, and there were no nipples livelier than hers, so firm, long and erect when aroused. "But it's more than chemistry," she said. "I'll let you in on a secret. Right before that time in New York, about two weeks earlier, I had a dream. I don't remember what it was all about except that I saw you in that dream. Your face—it came in so clear. I saw your face, Josh, and I hadn't even met you. Spooky?"

"What about what's-his-name?"

"He was a tryout. You're the real thing. You're Broadway."

I said, "Will we always be this mushy?"

"Oh yes. I will. I'll always be mushy about you. Sometimes I just want to swallow you up. I'm not talking sexually, although maybe that's the expression of it, you know, when I do that to you. But it's something else. Oh, you wouldn't understand."

I was reclining on the bed ready to go as she was finishing up in front of the mirror here in our cozy room in the Galaxy. I was feeling apprehensive and sluggish, and I wished, as I sometimes did, that everyone but Joan would go away. Sometimes she said the same thing—"If only there'd be just the two of us. No other women, especially. I resent other women."

"Getting late," I said.

"I'm ready," she said—which meant at least ten more minutes.

"How come a ponytail?"

"Because my hair's too long. What's wrong?"

"No, you look great. It's fine."

"I must get my hair cut when we get back to Philadelphia."

"You had to mention that word?"

"You're sure it's all right?"

"Women always worry about their hair. As if there were nothing else in the world."

"Here we go."

"It's true. On the subway that's all women talk about, their hair. Never politics or even sports. In the office, too, they all go around saying, 'Love your hair, Sue.' Why are all the girls in the office called Sue?"

"You're such a sexist!"

"I know. Isn't it wonderful?"

She threw something at me.

"Missed by a mile. Just like a woman."

Ibrahim was waiting for us in the lobby and he was also wearing white, just like Joan. Few men could get away with that, wearing an all-white suit, but he did and he looked stunning in it. His grin was so wide during the introductions that it seemed he had a thousand teeth.

"This is Joan," I said. "My wife."

He took her hand and bowed and she curtsied and people began to watch.

"This is Riva," he said.

I said "Hello, Riva," and she said nothing and I thought maybe I had insulted her.

"We have reservations at Il Verdi's in the Tropicana," Ibrahim said. "I hope that's agreeable."

"Oh that sounds wonderful," said Joan.

We had dined there once before, when I had won that three hundred dollars.

"So what are we waiting for?" I said.

"Yes, let's go," said Ibrahim. The restaurant was only a few blocks up the Boardwalk. We walked hurriedly as if the Trop were a train and we were rushing to catch it before it left. Il Verdi's was dark and candlelit. The women at the tables seemed glamorous, but none were like Joan; and none of the men were like Ibrahim.

We got seated in the best booth and Ibrahim ordered the wine.

He asked me if I had a cellar.

I said yes I did.

He talked about the winery he owned in France and I could not follow this too closely, all this talk of wine. He kept tossing out names and vintages. He knew all the good years and all the bad years and I did too, though I did not measure them by wine. He was not shy about his wealth, he was quite boastful in fact, but it suited that expansive personality.

He said, "Wine is one of the few things that improves with age. Wine and beautiful women."

I thought he'd raise his glass to Joan, but he didn't.

Anyway, we had all heard that line before and it was somewhat uncomfortable here in the beginning. All of it was superficially upbeat. There were lapses in conversation. There was the feeling, at least my feeling, that Ibrahim was *working*, like an insurance salesman with a pitch to make. Everything he said, even the small talk, and everything he didn't say seemed to be leading to something.

He was trying to make an impression and I had thought that burden would be on me.

When he was silent he seemed content to just sit and dominate, his tremendous physique and powerful head towering over the rest of us. His big dark eyes, so theatrical, did his talking for him. Now and then they landed on Joan. When they did she turned away. But sometimes she stared back.

When he spoke he confirmed my worst fears about this meeting. Never mind wineries, he owned buildings and ranches and stables of Arabian horses and cars and airplanes. He talked about all these, even about an island he half-owned. I wondered if I should mention my thirteen-year-old Malibu, which I owned outright.

"Life is good," he said. "We must remember that when we're sad."

Joan wasn't sad. She was as luminous as ever and kept shooting me happy glances. We both understood that this was another experience for our collective memory vault. These experiences we did own as nobody else, and for that we were wealthy beyond wineries and airplanes.

Now she said, "Is it true that you're a prince?"

Her attempt to be casual failed because there was no way to ask this question and not come across as schoolgirl innocent at the least, and at most downright starstruck.

But he saved her, saying, "We're all princes where I come from. Aren't they all princesses where you come from?"

She blushed and said, "Where is this place you come from, where you're all princes?"

"Somewhere in the Middle East."

"Oh. Am I being too forward? I happen to be a very curious person. I'm sorry."

"Please don't be." He turned to me. "But does it really matter where a person is from?"

"It does tell you half his story," I said.

"Yes, and I understand you also have a story, Joshua Kane. You were in Sinai, weren't you?"

"Yes—and I'm getting the feeling you know more about me than . . ."

"Don't trouble yourself about what I know, Joshua Kane, but tell me this—is it true about Dayan? They tell me he picked a spot where the Egyptian bombing was heaviest—stretched out and went to sleep. Bombs crashing all around and he slept. Can this be true?"

"Yes."

Ibrahim shook his head. "What a man he was. What a people you are. But I also come from a people. We trace ourselves back to 'the Amalekites, an ancient race and fearless."

"Also brutal. Good people for keeping a grudge."

The Amalekites were not my kind of folks. An ancient people all right. They had menaced the Hebrews at every turn. They were the sons of Esau-the-Redneck then, and they were the sons of Esau even today. Saul lost his kingship when he discarded the order to kill their king on account of that Hebrew failing, compassion.

At my rebuke Joan winced.

She knew I was long on patience, but not too long. She feared my dark side, as when a carload of white trash hassled us on the road and I let them race me over to the side and then proceeded to do what I had to do. She was impressed but unhappy. She said, "That look on your face! I never thought you could have that kind of look, and do such things." I said I had no choice. It was them or us. She understood, but she didn't understand. She didn't understand this either.

I used to tell her the whole world wasn't Bryn Mawr. She said neither was it Auschwitz.

Ibrahim now gave Joan a soft and tender gaze, and for me he had these slow, well-chosen words: "I keep no grudges, Mr. Kane. Only promises."

I felt myself gulp.

"Oh, and are you making a promise?"

"Perhaps."

"And what is this promise?"

He said, "Let that wait, Mr. Kane. That can wait."

Just in time to save a bad and worsening situation came Sy Rodrigo, PR man for the Galaxy and my buddy, going way back to the days when I was writing a newspaper column and he was a press agent for a Philadelphia night-club.

"Hey!" he said, giving it that showbiz flair and making a production of being astonished at seeing us here.

"Hey!" I said, and introduced him to Ibrahim and Riva, who really wasn't here or anywhere.

Sy was with a lady. He was in his mid-fifties, a man with a terrible complexion, the remnant of adolescent acne. Yet women were never a problem for Sy. He had already gone through two wives and had lived a life, mostly as publicist for entertainers, boxers, wrestlers, strippers and even big-time hoods, who paid him to keep their names out of the papers.

"What are you guys doing here?" he said. "I thought you belonged in my place."

"I could ask the same question, Sy."

"Me? Just checking out the competition. It's my job."

"Tough job."

"Yeah, but it's a living. How you doing, Josh?"

"All right. You?"

"Super."

"We're here as guests of Mr. Hassan."

"So I notice."

Sy noticed everything, and I never knew how to feel about the man. Sy was not a good person and Sy was not a bad person. Sy was Sy, promoter and opportunist with a sincere streak, but you could never be quite sure when it was sincere.

Everybody knew him and he knew everybody. PR was his business, people his product. He knew Philadelphia inside-out, Atlantic City upside-down. Even in New York he was no stranger.

He liked to brag that he could pick up a phone and get anybody, even the president.

He had no friends. He had pals.

In his business, favors—not money—were the medium of exchange. *You do me. I'll do you. Give me a mention in your column and I'll get you an interview with Frank.*

He said, "We could use your patronage at the Galaxy, Mr. Hassan. We're doing wonderful things."

"Ah yes," said Ibrahim.

"Give us a try."

Of course he meant the gaming tables.

I came to Ibrahim's rescue.

"Always working. Isn't that right, Sy."

"That's what it's all about."

His favorite line—*that's what it's all about.*

He said, "Got to run. Our table's ready. Stop up and say hello, Josh."

"Will do."

"Super."

I had the feeling, and this came to me after Sy left, that

Ibrahim and Sy did not have to be introduced. They knew one another. Nothing specific that I could point to. Just a feeling, and it did not have to mean anything, of course. Knowing the high-rollers, as Sy would say—that's what it's all about.

Now we were having our coffee and it was that part of the meal with strangers when you wonder if you'll ever be seeing them again—exactly how much of a fool have you made of yourself?

Ibrahim, since that timely intrusion from Sy, was back to being pleasant and talkative, and Joan was high, too.

"Do you gamble?" he asked her.

"No." Hair had fallen over her right eye and she gazed at him from profile and smiled.

"But of course you do," he said. "When you drive you gamble that every other motorist is sober. When you walk you gamble that you won't be mugged or attacked by a rabid dog. When you eat you gamble that your food is not poisoned. When you breathe you gamble that the air is not full of toxin. When you send your husband off to work you gamble that he won't be with another woman. A thousand times a day you gamble. Everything you do is a gamble. So what is it to put money on a horse or on cards? It's like anything else."

Joan was charmed. She said, "You're a persuasive man."

"Yes."

"And you've just turned me into a compulsive gambler. Just like that!"

Ibrahim tossed his head back in laughter. Not that Joan

had said anything so funny. No, he was merely expressing the delight of a man utterly satisfied with himself.
There was a tone of contemptuousness in the laughter as
well, the punishing sound of a winner, a winner in a
world of losers.

In fact, watching him now abandon himself so freely to
mirth, so mighty in his laughter . . . I could not help but
think, as if for the first time, that this was a world of
losers, all of us losers, and here was a winner. Here was a
winner.

"I may be compulsive myself," he said. "I gamble for
everything. Even for love."

"Huh!" said Joan, shifting in her seat and trying to
thwart his steady gaze.

He said, "With money, you know, everything is possible."

"No, that's not true," she said.

"Everything."

"Not true."

"Everything can be bought. Everything and everybody."

"Oh," said Joan, overly casual and nonchalant. "I suppose people can be bought?"

"Of course."

"Have you bought people?"

"For business, yes."

"For love?" she asked.

He gave this some thought. "Not yet."

"So there," said Joan. "You can't buy love."

"Oh, for the right price . . ."

"There is no price . . . love is . . ."

He held up his royal hand. "Please! I know *what love is.* I also know what money is."

He was being so candid that he even said something dangerously profound, that he had heard all the songs about love but if people were really honest they'd write more songs about money.

Said Joan, "What a pity."

"Pity?" he said.

"That you have to buy your way through life."

He laughed that big laugh.

"Touché. But you're wrong. It's called testing the limits. Women have a tough time understanding this."

Good and provoked, she snapped, "You'd be surprised what women understand."

"I certainly would be. Women lack . . . daring."

"Oh God!"

"Yes yes. Women lack daring. They're . . . predictable."

"Is that bad?"

"You tell me."

"I think . . . I think predictable can be bad, yes. But it can also be good. It depends. It depends on circumstances. It depends on the moment. Some moments, what's usually wrong might be right. Depends on what your feelings say."

He slapped the table and roared, "Then perhaps you are a daring woman!"

"Perhaps I am," she said coyly. "Perhaps I'm not."

I thought it so strange, how throughout all this Ibrahim kept ignoring his wife. This Riva, was she really alive? She refused to talk. So be it. Then again, Joan had done a fine job of excluding me, too.

Now Joan sensed this and said something about her husband the speechwriter. This prompted Ibrahim to say, "Just as you can't go to the bathroom for another man, so you can't write his speeches. But I am writing a book, Joshua Kane. Maybe you can help me."

I said everybody is writing a book.

"No," he said. "I'm serious."

I repeated that I only wrote speeches.

He said, "But when you started out, surely you intended to be a real writer."

This was unnecessary, especially in the presence of Joan.

She made a tactical blunder. She rushed to my defense. "Joshua," she said, "is the best at what he does."

Next time people defend me like this, I thought, I must remember to duck.

"I'm sure he is," Ibrahim said slowly.

"What's the book?" I said.

"I thought you'd never ask."

"I thought so, too," I said.

He already had the title. *"The Perfect Revenge.* Everybody has a story about getting even. We all want to get even with somebody—and some of us do. It can be quite fascinating. I want to put the best of these stories in a book. What do you think?"

"Sounds good."

"I mean these would have to be real stories about real people. You could do the research and even the writing, under my name, or we could use both our names. We should talk about this."

"But not now."

"I'm sure the book would get published," he said. "I own a publishing house."

We all laughed.

"In fact," he said, "that might be the first story. The man who owned the publishing company turned down another book I submitted. So I bought the company and fired the man. That's what I mean by revenge, Joshua Kane. His name was Cohen. That's what I mean by the perfect revenge."

I refused to return the look Joan gave me.

Ibrahim now said he had Jewish friends. Had even studied judo and karate under the famous Marcus Rosen. He modestly admitted to being a black belt, but *only* first Dan. Joan piped in that I had a brown belt in Krav Maga.

"You studied with Avri Ben Ish?" Ibrahim asked.

"For a time," I said. "In Pardes Chana."

"I've been there," he said. "I even met Imi in Natanya. You know him?"

"Yes, the father of Krav Maga. So you know Krav Maga, Mr. Hassan?"

"No," he said, "but they tell me it's the best system for hand-to-hand. After all, if the Israelis use it, it must be good. I'm always ready to learn. Maybe you can give me lessons."

"Or do you want to give me lessons, Mr. Hassan?"

"There's a boxing ring here we can use—if you like."

"You're challenging me?"

"I see you're not interested. Maybe some other time."

It occurred to me that I was already in a fight and that I was losing, but that was my style, in the beginning. I liked being underestimated, the underdog, even the scapegoat.

Frankly, unlike the Boy Scouts, I was never prepared. When I came under attack my first reaction was that the other person was only kidding. I always thought people were kidding. When I found out they weren't my question was, What have I done?

Usually, so far as I could tell, nothing.

But hang around long enough and you're bound to have done something to somebody.

This Ibrahim, I thought, is he kidding?

He said, "I did learn one classic Krav Maga hold. I wonder if I might show it to you."

He asked me if I knew the Cavalier, and of course I knew the Cavalier: grab hand and apply pressure to wrist to manipulate joint beyond normal range of motion.

In other words, terrific pain.

I had studied it in Pardes Chana and practiced it in Philadelphia under the second Dan black belt Alan Feldman, who had received it from Imi. Never failed to bring a man down, this hold. A grasp really, both hands of the attacker clasped together by the fingers, the defender's hand helplessly in between and one quick snap and it was over, broken wrist.

Or, it could be done slowly if your intention was merely to inflict pain and watch a man sink to his knees and beg.

I saw Ibrahim reach for my left hand. I could have

blocked him before he so much as touched me. Even once he held me I could have slipped out, in the early stages of the hold, by one of the six hand releases.

But no, I let him. This was all in fun, after all.

Though I was surprised . . . here, all this in public, out in the open.

So I let him grab me and as he did something changed in his eyes and his mouth went wide, showing at once the teeth of a smile and a grimace. A voice told me that I had made a mistake. We all make one mistake a day.

"I wish this weren't necessary," said Joan sternly and reprovingly. Her voice held a measure of fright and a hint of disgust and a dash of despair for all humanity. "This is stupid," she said, meaning the two of us, even though I had consented to play victim.

As to why I had—good question. Strange generation, this generation that I belonged to, that in a single lifetime had seen both the dream of Hitler and the dream of Herzl come true, and only about a half decade apart.

Bound to create hybrids of men, men still unsure of who to follow, Akiba or Bar Kochba.

But there was a choice, finally, and for now I had chosen this.

So he locked my hand between his "69"-shaped palms, perfect Cavalier form, and went to work. Slowly at first, but my ears were already beginning to ring. Then he began the twisting, clockwise from one o'clock to two to three to four to five to six to seven, my wrist going one way, my palm the other, violating the delicate balance of the human anatomy.

Forget pain. I was already up to grief.

"Stop it!" Joan said, unaware that we were gone, departed from her world. Into our own place of sands and tents and camels and wadis and nomads and the weeping women.

Riva sat there impassively.

Ibrahim picked up more power from the leverage of his body, inclining me ever more downward.

His fingers now were flaming tongs and all right, I thought, he knows the hold, and it's time to say so, except this: they are watching from the hills of Hermon to the springs of En-Gedi.

So I let him take me to eight o'clock and even nine and then, then I tapped my leg, the signal among gentlemen and martial artists that the limit of pain had been achieved—I tapped my leg and instead he took me to ten.

"Hey!" I said, my face down down down and sweat pouring from my entire body. The heat!

Again I tapped my leg and he was laughing and took me up to eleven.

"Stop it!" said Joan.

He notched me up to twelve and now . . . now it was unbearable.

I tapped my leg, again and again, and soon there'd be no strength even for that anymore.

"Enough!" said Joan. "Enough!"

Riva—I thought this might be the time for her to wake up and say something. I looked at her and she even looked back but with absolutely no expression. I wasn't *here* for her. I now realized this: No man or woman existed for her except Ibrahim. He was more than perfection in her eyes. He was creation.

"Am I doing it right?" he said.

"Enough!" said Joan.

"Am I doing it right?"

"Enough!"

"Just tell me if I'm doing it right."

But I couldn't mouth the words.

"For God's sake, you're doing it right," said Joan.

Now he offered the release and just like that we all began to laugh. I was all right. Excellent.

"Good?" said Ibrahim.

"Oh yes," I said.

"Your Imi would be proud?"

Not of me, I thought. Not of me.

Then again, maybe yes. I remembered Imi that day in Natanya by the sea, sharing cheese cake with him at the Ugati around a Parisian-style outdoor table. He was lecturing us on the essence of serenity. He straightened himself erect in his chair, cast his eyes far off into the depths of the Mediterranean, held his fists tucked to his waist, and said, "While everyone around you is jumping and hopping and doing this and doing that . . . you . . . you sit. You *sit*. You make your place not here, but there, away. You sit. Like this. Like this. You see? Like this."

So now I sat there like this but said to myself, *Remember. Do not forget.*

CHAPTER
7

WE LEFT IBRAHIM and Riva behind for a husband-and-wife stroll on the Boardwalk. Ibrahim had invited us to join him in the casino but I was not in the mood and neither was Joan. Joan had turned peevish. Something had happened. As for me, too much sun in the morning and Ibrahim at night.

The heavens were lit and to our right, as we walked, the ocean was splendid in its everlasting murmur. To our left we passed Fun Spot Arcade, Ice Cream Parlour, Jackpot Souvenir Shop, Pier 21 T-Shirt Factory, Reader and Advisor and A. L. Roth's candy and nut shop, all anachronisms against the gambling strongholds of Bally's Grand, the Versailles, Tropicana, the Galaxy, Atlantis, Trump Plaza, Caesar's, Bally's Park Place, the Claridge, the Sands, all the way to Resorts and Showboat.

In the old days the six-mile Boardwalk had been an esplanade second only to the ocean as a resort feature. The rich and the weekend rich used to parade in their finery. Now the casinos were everything, and the people who played in them stayed in them, and the Boardwalk was left largely to the dregs who washed up from the interior and from the bus depot on Arctic Avenue.

Right here in what Boardwalk veterans remembered as Chelsea, here along the railing, the leisure class sat in their parked rolling chairs, the men fat and bald and smoking cigars, and the women clothed in mink stoles, munching polly seeds and spitting the shells all over the wooden planks.

People danced in those days and wore evening gowns and ate at Sid Hartfield's or Kent's, and they stayed at the Ambassador, the Marlboro-Blenheim, the Brighton, the Breakers.

Even the language was different. The word wasn't *glitzy*. It was *ritzy*.

The place we were now passing, Ocean One, a sprawling shopping mall built over the waters, had once been Million Dollar Pier, where people danced to the music of Eddie Morgan.

But I still loved it here, everything about the place.

"Did you have a nice time?" I asked Joan after some silence.

She did not answer—so meditative.

"I purposely made it simple. Yes you did, no you didn't. Yes or no."

Still nothing.

"All right. Blink once for yes, twice for no."

"He propositioned me," she said.

I stopped dead. She kept on walking. I rushed up.
"What?"

"You heard me."

"How?"

"He asked me to go to bed with him. That's how."

"When?"

"While you were talking to Sy."

"But that was only a second."

"That's all it takes."

"What did you say?"

Now she stopped.

"What do you think I said?"

"I don't know."

"You don't know?"

"I would hope . . ."

Her right hand came flashing and caught me on the left side of my face. Then she ran off and I followed slowly behind. I lost sight of her when she turned to the doors of the Galaxy. I got there a few minutes later, took the elevator up, and she was in the shower when I walked in. Yes, she needed a shower.

I sat down on the bed. I felt nothing, a calm to cover a fright.

"I'm sorry," she said when she came out.

"So am I."

"Did I hurt you?"

"Not as much as I hurt you. Forgive me."

"Let's just choose our friends more carefully from now on."

"He's no friend of mine," I said.

"He actually expects me to be at his suite tomorrow at six."

"I'll be there instead."

"No you won't. It's over."

"No it isn't."

"Josh, a man propositioned me. I feel cheap and filthy—but nothing happened. Don't complicate things."

"Something smells," I said.

"What?"

"I don't know. But I've got to find out."

"We have to remember that this is a very wealthy man. His values are not our values."

"What exactly did he say?"

"Josh . . ."

"I have to know."

"He said, 'Let's make love. My place tomorrow at six.' Okay?"

"What did you say?"

"Nothing."

"Nothing? You mean you were thinking?"

"No, I was trying to make a joke of it, think of something funny to say."

"So what *did* you say?"

"I said no. Of course I said no. Josh, if I didn't love you so much I'd hate you right now."

"I hate myself. I got you into this."

"Okay, so now I'm out."

I got up and held her close and firm. So often that embrace resolved our conflicts. This time we both stepped back empty. She was not even crying; she was too disgusted or too *something* to cry.

Now wait a minute, I thought. No one's been raped or anything. A man made a play for my wife. Right under my nose. Disgusting, yes, but not tragic, and certainly not irreversible. *Nothing happened,* as Joan said.

But maybe something did happen.

"Were you tempted?" I asked.

"Absolutely not."

"*Are* you tempted now?"

"Josh—why are you doing this?"

"I feel jealous as hell."

"About what?"

"That he's got you wondering."

"I am not wondering. Leave it alone, Josh. It's getting dangerous."

How deftly he had moved, I thought. I had not even noticed him talking to Joan while I had been talking to Sy. How long had this been in the works anyway? From the time he first saw her in the lobby this evening, or gradually over dinner?

Then again, *was* this the first time he had seen her? Maybe he'd seen her before. Strange, I thought, how Sy just happened to pop in. No, Sy had nothing to do with this. That was going too far.

Right, a man had made a play for my wife. I should not be so astonished. She is, I thought, an extraordinarily beautiful woman. After all, I too had made a play for her when she had belonged to another, and won her. Yes, that would always be with me. If I could steal her, so could someone else.

His values, as she said, are not our values. But what are our values? We had once cheated. Those were not our values. So we had made a deal. We had agreed that we were not really cheating because we were so much in love.

So much in love that it had to be right. Once we were married we'd return to our values and settle into old-fashioned middle-class fidelity. That was the deal and the deal was still valid.

This—this was different. This was not love. This was an attempted seduction.

Joan was still mine.

But there was doubt. There had to be doubt.

She hadn't said no right away. She had paused. Doubt, in her mind, in his mind, in my mind.

Finally, she let it go. Tears flowed down her cheeks.

"Don't you know," she said, "that I love you more than anything? Even if I was tempted—and I wasn't—I'd never do anything to ruin what we have. I'm yours, Joshua, fully and always. Nothing can come between us. Nothing. Do you understand?"

CHAPTER
8

THE NEXT MORNING we had breakfast again in the Galaxy Coffee Shoppe, facing the Boardwalk and the ocean. It was pleasant, the atmosphere of the place. We talked about the weather, how fortunate we were to have it so hot and sunny.

But Joan was not going to the beach today. Maybe, she said, she'd sit by the pool, indoors.

"You can join me," she said, "or play blackjack all day."

I was as flat as she was. I did not feel like going to the beach either, or to the pool, and I did not feel much like gambling. Suddenly there was nothing to do.

The waitress brought over our eggs and toast.

"I ordered an English muffin," Joan told the waitress, in a tone void of her usual charm.

The waitress apologized, scooped up the plate with toast and said she'd be back with the English muffin. By the time she came back, the eggs were cold. She then offered to take back the eggs, but then the English muffin would be cold.

The situation seemed hopeless—about the way we were feeling about everything this morning.

"Never mind," said Joan. "I'll just eat this the way it is."

But she didn't. She only sipped coffee.

"I'm on a diet anyhow," she said.

I stared out the window to hide from her cheerlessness—and from what had gone on between us last night.

Something told me that Joan had grown up overnight. She had avoided adulthood until now, and now it had rushed up on her.

"I feel that I've lost you," she finally said.

"Never."

"Just listen. Don't talk. I feel that I've lost you. But I'll win you back. Let's just get over this vacation without further damage. Okay? That's what we have to do. Survive this vacation. You don't trust me. I know. You never did. But I will win your trust. It will take time. Years. But I'll win your trust as I once won your love. One thing at a time."

She had forbidden me to talk, so I said nothing. I stared out the window.

"I know what you're thinking," she said. "In that Biblical mind of yours you imagine God cooking up all kinds of mischief to get even with us. Because we'd been unfaithful ourselves. Well we're not unfaithful now and we're never going to be and if your God is not a God of forgiveness, then he is not my God. My God is loving and forgiving. We're good people, Josh. Don't be waiting for retribution. We're good people."

Yes we are, I thought. We're good people. Except are there any people out there who think they're bad?

"Let's forget about it," she said by way of reminding me and bringing back all the quivers of last night.

"It's forgotten."

"Good," she said.

Silence. We took turns avoiding glances.

"Totally forgotten," I said.

"So let's not talk about it anymore."

"Talk about what? I've forgotten."

She smiled and the magic was back, almost.

"You're such a . . ."

"Such a what?"

"Such a guy."

"You were flirting, you know."

I couldn't help it, it just came out.

"Flirting?" she said. "Flirting? Flirting? I was flirting?"

"Flirting. You were flirting."

"I can't believe you're saying this, Josh."

"Neither can I."

"I never flirt . . . except with you."

"Maybe I'm wrong."

"Dead wrong."

"Aha."

She said, "I was wrong on one thing. When I said you're the best at what you do. That was stupid. But he was disparaging you. The way he tried to degrade you . . . I couldn't just sit there and say nothing."

"Didn't bother me."

"Well it bothered me. I'm so proud of what you do, and

♠ 83 ♠

you *are* the best speechwriter in the world, and nobody knows it, not even you. I don't know how you do it, write these speeches for these big executives, and never get a word of recognition."

"It's okay."

"You do all the work and they get all the credit. They should say, 'This speech was written by Joshua Kane.' "

Couldn't help but laugh.

Once, the CEO of a Fortune 500 company had given an inspired talk to the chamber of commerce on the topic of "We're Part of a World Economy." He was interrupted twelve times by applause, and in the end they gave him a standing ovation.

I was there, in the back, and so was Joan. I had made the mistake of bringing her along.

She said, "Isn't he going to mention you?"

"Of course not."

"Those were all your words."

"Shh."

"Is it always like this?"

"It's the way it's supposed to be."

"This is a crime."

Now I said, "So I'm modest. What's wrong with modesty?"

"Aren't you the one who says everything in moderation?"

"Even moderation," I said.

"That's my point."

"What's your point?"

"Too much modesty," she said, "is a form of conceit."

"That's a hell of a statement."

"You have nothing to show for anything you've ever done, Josh. Do you realize that?"

"I have you."

"Sweet, Josh. But I know you won a batting title in college. Hit .400, didn't you?"

"Hit .406, like Ted Williams. How did you know?"

"Because they're still sending you letters to pick up your trophy."

"College baseball doesn't count."

"Yes it does count," she said. "Everything counts. Didn't you win something like the Medal of Honor for those wars in Israel?"

"I've got medals. You even complain about them."

"No I don't. But anyway, where's the big one?"

"Somewhere."

"You're making a statement, Josh."

"Uh-oh."

"Yes, this is what you're saying . . ."

"I don't want to hear."

"You're saying, 'I am nobody!' "

"To the contrary, my dear. I need no medals to verify me."

"You're like your father. Very strong when it comes to standing up for other people."

"Isn't that good?"

"Yes, but you've never learned to stand up for yourself. I'll tell you why. It's the immigrant in you."

"I'm as American as you."

"You don't think you belong. You're afraid to be

noticed—they'll deport you or something. You're afraid to own things because you'll only have to leave them behind. Yes, Josh, it's true, and for the same reason you were jealous of . . . of that Arab."

No more arguments from me, I thought—at least for now—against this lady's powers of deductive reasoning. Straight from the schools of Aristotle, her favorite Greek.

Moments like these we were mind for mind, heart for heart, soul for soul, and it was so obvious that we were meant for each other that it was strange to think that other people fell in love, too.

She was probably right about everything. This gift of perception, it was a delight. Knowing the truth, even the hidden truth of things, and saying the right things at the right time. She knew moment and timing. She lit bells inside the brain as when she said everything counts. Profound. To me, profound. On our wedding night, that toast—"May we continue to enrich each other's lives."

We were still doing that—but no doubt about it, she had been flirting.

CHAPTER
9

SY's OFFICE was on the fifth floor of the Galaxy—part of an executive and administrative complex set off from the casino below and the hotel rooms above. Sy's place was the business hub.

When I walked in Sy was on the phone, as usual. He was telling someone that backrubs were not part of her contract, and besides, the masseur was out sick.

A famous comedian was already in Sy's office, and when Sy hung up the man said: "I just can't do it, Sy."

"It took all the pull I had to get you on that show. I thought you wanted the publicity."

"I don't need fucking publicity. You calling me a has-been?"

"I'm not calling you a thing. *We* need the publicity, okay?"

"I don't need this dump, you know. I can work Vegas for twice the money."

"Hey, there's no need for this."

"Yeah, you said it," said the famous comedian and stomped out.

"Funny man," I said.

"Laugh a minute. Welcome to the end of the world, old buddy. Enjoying yourself? Joan looks great. You, you don't look so good. We taking good care of you? If not, just let me know. I just can't get you a backrub, that's all, and I can't get you on 'Good Morning America.' Did you see that guy? Our star attraction this weekend. Begging me to get him on 'Good Morning America.' So I get him on—and it wasn't easy, he is a has-been, you know—and what does he do? Finks out on me.

"He's not a has-been for nothing. The smaller they are, I say, the smaller they are. The girl, his co-star, she wants a backrub. Can't go on without a backrub. Ever seen such babies? They're all babies. Everything's an emergency with them. Around here every minute it's the end of the world. But you know that already. So what can I do for you?"

"This man Ibrahim," I said, "do you know him?"

A woman in a serious business suit stepped in and said, "The tee-shirt ad ran with the wrong dates."

"Can't you run a new ad?"

"We'll get a make-good but meanwhile we'll need something, a news release if you can get one out."

"I'll see what I can do."

"ASAP," she said on her way out.

"Tee-shirts," said Sy. "Yes?"

His secretary was at the door.

"Lady here says she was assaulted by one of our bus drivers."

Sy shook his head.

"That's a security problem. Take her to security."

"She's very upset."

"You mean she wants a comp. Give her a buffet. But first take her to security." Again, the two of us alone, Sy said, "So what can I do for you?"

The phone rang. "You say your name is what?" Sy asked the caller. "And you're from what paper? I see. Well send us your request by mail, on New York *Times* stationery, and we'll give it our consideration. Frankly, no, I never heard of you. But then, there are many people I never heard of. Same to you." He hung up and said, "Another reporter from the *Times*. Wants comped room and meals for a *week*. He's from the *Times* like I'm from the *Times*. So what can I do for you?"

"This man Ibrahim, do you know him?"

"Of course I know him. I know all the high-rollers. That's my job. Very rich man. By last count he was worth three billion, I said *billion* dollars. He's a sultan of some sort. Runs his own country, where it rains oil. Mahareen, I think it's called, somewhere outside of Iraq. Population about eighty thousand. They're all cousins. His father was even more wealthy than Ibrahim. Killed in a coup, his father. The coup, between you and me, might have been Ibrahim. Tough man . . . but educated in all the best European schools. Learned flawless American English in Texas. Spent two years there in military training. Top secret. He lost an eye in a war. Could you tell?"

"No," I said.

"Don't ask me what war. They're always having wars, as you know. Holy wars, no less. That woman with him is his wife. I hear he has more back home. Riva is Spanish. Spanish girl. Never says a word, as you've noticed. Beautiful but dumb, and I mean dumb in the literal sense. But that's how they train their women out there in the Middle East. We should only have it so good, know what I mean?"

"I'd go crazy with a woman like that," I said.

"I guess you're right. I'd go crazy, too. So does he, in fact. He's got a roving eye. Like Freud, American women turn him on. Loves blondes. Aren't too many blondes out there in the desert. But I've never known him to make a real play."

I have, I thought.

Sy gave me a suspicious look when he said that. Or maybe I just thought he did.

"He collects antique cars," Sy continued. "Champion polo player. Plays chess. Very good, I understand. Also plays bridge, enters the tournaments. Your basic all-Mahareen billionaire, you know? Comes here once a year for the delights of our town. A Moslem, but drinks when he's here. Very active in Arab causes but doesn't hate Jews. Why?"

"Well you know we got acquainted," I said.

"The whole town knows. Everybody knows about that scene at the Versailles. Did he at least give you pocket money for your troubles? Like maybe fifty, and I mean thousand?"

"No, but of course we had dinner. I introduced you and you acted like strangers."

"That was etiquette. It's presumptuous to *know* a sultan. What's up?"

"Nothing."

"He's no phony, if that's what you're thinking. He's been known to drop three million in a single night—and walk away as if nothing happened. Why not? While he's taking a piss his oil wells are recouping that loot. We've been trying to get him here for years but he refuses to play at our tables. If he and his cousins brought their business here we wouldn't be chasing after the tee-shirt trade. Know what I mean?"

"He's never been here?" I asked.

Sy did not like the question.

"He *was* here once."

"When?"

"Couple of days ago in fact. Walked in, looked around, walked out. Didn't like the feel of the place, I guess. Gamblers go by feel, especially high-rollers, and this man is a high-roller, the highest of the high. Ever have so much money that you can't lose? Even when you lose you win?"

"No, Sy. I never had that kind of money."

"That's the thing about this guy. Even when he loses he wins. Is life fair?"

"For him it is."

"Yeah, but not altogether. No man has everything, as we all know. He's a diabetic. Takes insulin. A doctor travels with him wherever he goes. Part of a very large retinue. You never see them but don't kid yourself, they're there. Tell you the truth, Josh, I was surprised, I mean about you and him getting together. I know you fought against them in sixty-seven. I remember how you rushed off to Israel. You're a flaming Zionist, Joshua."

"I don't hate Arabs, Sy. I only hate them when they hate me."

"Spoken like a true Christian. Anything else?"

No, I thought. Nothing else. Though I still knew nothing about the man Ibrahim. Except for some bio information. There was more to him than that, and less, for sure.

He was not invincible. He had all the money in the world but only one eye, and for all his power and good looks he had diabetes. So he was not perfect, and in that case I had a chance.

I had to know that so that I could subdue him, in some way diminish him in Joan's eyes. Despite her protests, Ibrahim, the *romance* of Ibrahim, would remain with her even if the man himself departed. Unless I could find the means to rout him. No, Ibrahim would not simply vanish, and I could not allow him to disappear into the Arabian desert carrying Joan's heart. I had to deal with him here, while he was still reality—and before he could escape and become her fantasy.

I asked Sy how important it was to the Galaxy to have a man like Ibrahim play at its tables.

"Very important," he said. "Very, very important. That's what it's all about."

I asked him what the Galaxy would do to snare a man like Ibrahim.

"Anything—you name it," he said.

I did not know what to name, but I could think of a few things.

Sy explained that the Galaxy had never been a place for high-rollers. The Versailles, Caesar's, Resorts, Trump's—

those were the places. But plans were in the works to draw "quality players" to the Galaxy.

To the Galaxy's new top man, Roy Stavros, that was priority number one. Architects were already designing separate quarters for hundred-dollar-minimum tables— red drapes, chandeliers, dealers in tuxedos and a hostess for every single player, whatever his whim might be.

Yes, anything—anything and everything for the high-roller.

What would Sy—my friend Sy—what would *he* do to snare the high-rollers? I didn't ask.

But he seemed to have heard the unasked question.

"We're all prostitutes, Josh. You know that. You weren't born yesterday."

Sy had always been fair with me. When I had quit newspapering for the more lucrative speechwriting, he had been there, years ago, to remind me that it was all right—I had not sold out. His way of saying that I had.

Survival, he had said, that's what it's all about. We'll do anything to survive. Flesh will eat flesh to survive.

On that I never agreed with him. We'll do our utmost to survive—but not anything.

Now I said, "Oh come on, Sy. We're not prostitutes, not all of us. Not even most of us."

Sy laughed.

"Such innocence," he said. "In this age! From an ex-news guy yet! Don't you know what goes on? I guess not. In this business at least, we buy people every day. We bring them in by bus, by limo, by plane. We house them. We feed them. We booze them. We baby them. What we're doing, Josh—what we're doing is buying them. People are *vulnerable*, Josh, and I'll tell you why. They're vulnerable because everybody wants something *better.* You hear that? Everybody wants something better out of life. Nobody, nobody is happy with what he's got. That's why we prosper here in this business. We cater to that, to that weakness, to that weakness in *everybody*—even the Ibrahims of the world."

He was giving me the speech he could never write for his own boss, sharing the inner truths that a company PR guy had to swallow, though it was not altogether certain whether he was speaking from rage or from pride or a mixture of both, and he continued: "That's right, Josh. Everybody thinks he's been cheated by life. You know that, Josh. You're no kid. We all think we've been gypped. Nobody's happy with his lot in life, and you know the saying, 'Who is rich? He who is happy with what he's got.' Is anybody?

"You know and I know that nobody but *nobody* is happy with what he's got. It's never enough. Even people who have it all don't have enough, and let's face it, most people really do have nothing. Nothing is a big word but you know what I mean.

"So it's a beautiful situation, don't you see? I mean for those of us in this business. We'll never go broke and if a particular casino does go in the red it's strictly mismanagement because the people are out there, all of them seeking this elusive thing, which, like I said, is a *better* life.

"*Something better,* Josh. *Something better.* That's the human cry.

"Animals, too, for your information. Animals run, birds fly, fish swim upstream for miles and miles because *there* is better than here. Instinct—the pursuit of something better. Even a fish thinks his creator done him wrong.

"People, it's true, don't wise up so fast, so you'll notice most of our clientele is middle-aged. That's no coincidence, Josh. The young, they still think there's a whole life ahead.

"Later they find out, hey, my life's half over and what's this? What have I got? This isn't right. This isn't *fair*. I've been *cheated*. I've got *better* coming to me, and so here they are, Josh—watch them at the tables, watch them at the slots.

"Look at their faces and tell me, are they playing? Are they? They're not playing. This isn't games. This isn't even fun. This is serious. Seen anybody smile at blackjack or baccarat or the slots?

"Ever seen anybody take in our lounge acts? We bring in the best, and for what?"

"Fun," I said. "People come here to have fun."

Sy laughed. "Yeah, fun-in-the-sun. Listen, we've got people coming here who don't even know there's an *ocean* across the street. Yeah. Oh we sell it as fun, the whole package. You've seen our ads, and there is that element of fun, but it's serious, Josh, too serious.

"Had one guy here the other day playing way way over his head at the roulette. I mean this guy was going through torture, losing bundle after bundle, sweating and swearing. Never seen a guy so miserable. Up comes his father, tugs his sleeve, you know, to pull him away, to tell him to leave some money for the wife and kids. This guy wheels around and says, 'Leave me alone, Dad. Can't you see I'm having *fun?*'

"Take it from me, Josh. The word is *vulnerable.* That's where we come in.

"The guy who invented gambling . . . what a genius! He knew just where to tap in.

"That's us. We put out the bait. We say here it is, come and get it, win that million dollars, and they come. They come with a vengeance.

"Here's a number for you—*thirty million.* That's how many people hit the casinos here during the course of a year. There's no other place on earth that gets that many people. Thirty million. Do that many people go to church?"

I said if all the world's churches were in one place, you'd get your thirty million.

He said, "Not on your life. People have given up on religion. Oh they go to church to pay their respects, but that's out of fear. Just in case there is a God. But you don't need *faith* to believe in a slot machine. Just take a bus and there it is. Just pull the handle and, who knows, you may never again have to *pray* for a better life.

"Because that's what we do here Josh, we promise a better life, the thing we're all after, even you. True, we *spend* all kinds of money, but there's a reason. More money! We'll spend a million bucks to move a staircase from here to there because why? Because in the end it'll bring us in a million bucks more. The point is this: in the casino business money is first, last and everything in between. Up and down the Boardwalk we're all in the business of *buying* people. Sometimes all it takes is a tee-shirt. Sometimes it takes more. But I've never met the man, or woman, who could not be bought. We're just talking price."

CHAPTER
10

A PRIVATE ELEVATOR, hidden from public view, shot up to the suites of the very rich. It was in a secluded corner, in a room that served as a graveyard for dead slot machines.

I had been directed to it by the Versailles's bell captain, who had first made a phone call, mentioning my name. So Ibrahim knew I was coming. Instead of Joan.

Now I pressed the button for the elevator and when it came for me I had second thoughts, as always. Elevators were not my favorite pastime. I had no fear of heights, or of flying, or even of combat or any of the other usual things, but elevators terrified me.

Being *closed in!* Worse, being *forgotten*—yes, that was my biggest fear. Someday I'd be stuck in an elevator and nobody would know. For hours, days, weeks, months, years. Nobody would miss me enough to know or care. Being forgotten. I could think of nothing more dreadful.

Being dead would not be half as bad—if people knew you were dead. But suppose you were dead and people didn't even know you were dead? That would be awful.

Suppose you were alive and people didn't even know you were alive? That would be worse—the worst.

In the elevator, riding up to number eighteen, I thought of what to say. Stop propositioning my wife? That wouldn't go. I thought of what to do. Challenge him to a duel? That was outdated. So I really had no plan, other than to show up and satisfy—more than curiosity. Something much more than curiosity.

I did have doubts about whether I was doing the right thing. Joan and I had quarreled most of the afternoon about this. She thought I was being foolish. "The old macho thing," she had said. She had also said something else. "You can't win against a man like that." Close to what Sy had said—*Even when the man loses he wins. He cannot lose.* That did trouble me now, that thought.

When I stepped off the elevator a man who looked like Paul Newman—though I'm sure he wasn't—welcomed me by saying, "Follow, please." I detected an accent other than Arabic.

Apart from the Paul Newman resemblance, I recognized this man. Then I remembered that I had seen him the night before at an adjoining table while the four of us were dining in the Trop.

Soon other faces began to appear in the corridors as I followed Paul Newman—familiar faces. It became clear to me that Ibrahim did indeed have a retinue, and they *were* everywhere.

I was escorted to a room that surprised me for its lack of decor. There was a beige sofa, twin chairs, a coffee table and a bar. Of course this was but one of many rooms, for

Ibrahim had the whole floor to himself. Besides, maybe Ibrahim liked his rooms spare. A rich man did not have to be *rich* all the time, as opposed to a poor man, who had to be poor all the time.

I was left alone for some time. Was I being watched? I thought I was. In fact, I'd had that sensation even in the elevator, and even before that on the Boardwalk, walking over. Paranoid, maybe. Maybe not.

Ibrahim strolled in wearing his black suit and white smile. Women would no doubt call him dashing. Now he was so jovial that by impulse I got up from my chair and shook his extended hand. We were alone in the room. He offered me a Manhattan and made himself a cognac.

"I knew you'd come," he said and when he sat down, facing me, I noticed a peculiar gesture. Rather than hitch up his pants by the knee as some men do to save the crease, he needlessly made a crosswise motion with his right hand, a sign that at home he wore flowing robes.

The Sultan of Mahareen!

"Not my wife?" I said.

"No, I expected you, and I'm so glad you came. We have much to talk about."

"You have interesting bodyguards," I said.

"Oh?"

"They're Israeli, aren't they?"

He stilled a cough, as close as he'd ever come to expressing astonishment.

"Excellent," he said. "How did you know?"

"The accents. And not one of them is wearing a tie."

"Are you surprised?"

"No. King David's bodyguards were Philistines. In a man's palace his enemies are to be trusted more than his friends."

"But surely you wonder how such an arrangement came about."

"Yes, I do wonder."

"Then I'll tell you. On the surface, for the sake of Arab unity, my country is in a perpetual state of war with Israel. We say all the right things against them, for public consumption, and don't even recognize their right to exist. The reality is different. We're friends. Not for love, perhaps—though I find them good people—but for necessity. We both live on dry land. They have no oil. We have no water. We send them our oil. They send us their drip-irrigation experts. Of such necessities friendships are made, Mr. Kane, even in times of war. The same can be said for individuals, like the two of us. All I have to do is find your necessity. You already know mine."

"Am I expected to be civil after a remark like that?"

"Yes, because we're talking business."

"We are?"

"I'm prepared to understand that your wife will continue to spurn me. That's why I'm talking to you."

"Business," I said.

"Business," he said. "Business is two people exchanging necessities."

"My wife is not business, Mr. Hassan."

"Oh everything is business, Mr. Kane. Everything is a transaction. Everything is business and I will show you how. *I am offering you one million dollars for one night with your wife.*"

And a camel to be named later?

Okay, I thought, this is the most stunning moment of your life, Joshua Kane. The rudest compliment! Has any man ever been so insulted? Has any man ever been so flattered? What can be higher? What can be lower?

"One night and one night only," Ibrahim continued. "One million dollars. Tax free."

I laughed and said something stupid: "I've never heard of anything like this!"

"I have never seen anything like your wife, Mr. Kane. That makes it even odds. That makes it business."

"Never."

"Please, I'm not asking you to decide now. Think it over. Think of the million dollars. But remember . . . the night will come and go. The money lasts a lifetime. So don't say never, Mr. Kane. It's something to think about."

I got up and put my drink down. That was the problem—something to think about.

"So soon?" he said. "I thought you were a gambler, Mr. Kane. Well here it is. The jackpot! For what? The stakes are not so high. A million dollars is nothing to me. One night with your wife—that should be nothing to you. *One* night."

"I don't gamble my wife."

"Gambling is gambling. Your wife herself agreed she is a compulsive gambler. So this is one more gamble."

"When did you first see my wife?"

"Together with you on the casino floor of the Galaxy."

♠   103   ♠

"Does Sy Rodrigo have anything to do with this?"

"Very little. I did ask him to identify you—you and your beautiful wife."

"So you already knew me when you asked me to join you at the Versailles table for good luck."

"Yes, I already knew you, and yes, I befriended you for this purpose."

He was obviously prepared to slay me with candor.

"Does Sy know anything about this offer?"

"I did not mention it to him. But Sy Rodrigo is nobody's fool."

"Yes, he's a man who lives by the verities of clichés. He believes every man can be bought. The only issue is price, and you're offering me a million dollars. Tell me, Mr. Hassan, did you promise to play at his tables in exchange for the sacrifice of my wife? Was that the deal?"

"There was no deal. Perhaps an understanding, and why do you say sacrifice? I am not going to kill her. We're only talking, well, since we are being frank, we're only talking sex. You've already had many nights with her and you'll have many more. I'm only asking for one. Are you afraid she'll fall in love with me?"

"No, but I am disgusted with myself for even hearing you out."

"Yes, you have your pride, your integrity, your values. But you do not have a million dollars!"

"No money is enough for what you're asking."

"So you say now. But I assure you you'll give it thought. I guarantee, in fact, that that's all you'll think about."

I picked up my drink and sat down again. Somewhere

there was the perfect response to all this but I could not call it in. I sought a phrase or a dramatic gesture to bring this thing to a conclusion, now, in this room, before it got out and became the fixation of my days. But I was witless.

I had stupidly walked into a world where I could not win. Even if I won I lost. Just as the reverse was true with him. Even if he lost he won. As Joan had said. As Sy had said. Right, this was a man who could not lose.

In his world there were no limits. In my world there were nothing but limits.

At the blackjack table I had had my first insight into how a man of incredible wealth could turn everything upside down, could cheapen even the priceless. Like an idiot I had stepped right in, into where duty of man to God, honor of man to man, fidelity of man to woman, were a mockery in the shadow of a mountain that loomed even larger than Sinai.

Yes, people were vulnerable because everybody wants something better. That was what Ibrahim had seen in me. I thought I had been so cool there as his partner in blackjack, but he had sniffed out my hunger, even my desperation. He had the measure of me, which was to say that, in his eyes, I was like the rest, a piddling creature, pathetic for his yearnings.

Now it was too late to turn back. The discussion itself, the fact that I was partaking, already made me an accomplice—already tarnished me and certainly Joan. Like it or not, I had anted up and I was in.

"I guarantee you that I will not think about it," I said remembering that doubt, hesitation, was the wedge he sought, the wedge he had found when Joan had failed to rebuff him promptly. Only yesterday, I thought, he had tried her for free.

"Perhaps," he said, "Joan will want to think about it, and I do hope you will bring it up with her."

"If I don't?"

"If you don't, I will."

"Your arrogance, sir, is . . ."

"If you intend to insult me you're wasting your time, Mr. Kane. I expect you to be outraged. But I also expect you to be reasonable and open-minded. I have made you an offer. You have no choice but to accept. Think of the gains. You're losing nothing. Sex? We live in an age where sex is nothing. Something else, Mr. Kane. Sooner or later Joan will have an affair with another man. I assure you she will. I know her type. She is too beautiful for one man. So why not now and make a profit?"

At that phrase in particular I should have been wildly offended. But I wasn't. I was charmed, as awful as that is to admit. Charmed by his reasoning, his candor, his talent for reducing the complex to the simple. What's more, the smile never left his face, a smile that somehow brought us together under the same joke.

He was serious, of course. But he left room for humor, enough humor to keep me sharing his disdain for my world. I envied him. Not his money. But to be so impervious to the treasures of middle-class values was a freedom to be coveted.

His eyes clung to me—and I still did not know which one was made of glass. To make a point he'd sometimes get up from his chair and tower over me, though not menacingly. He moved with the grace of an athlete, powered by the assurance of self-adulation. He loved himself, and that too was charming.

If you stripped him of his mystique—which was tough to do—he was a spoiled child and nothing more. Surely he had never been denied even the most outlandish fancy. If he wanted something, he got it. If he wanted something that belonged to someone else, he got that too.

So it was when you were the Sultan of Mahareen, where it rained oil—and blessings came to the blessed. His wealth was not only in money but also in dangerous good looks. In his desert kingdom he was certainly known as God's Beloved.

Now he leaned back in his chair, crossed his legs, made that royal motion over his pants again, and gave me his most mischievous smile yet.

"Suppose I suffered from Jake Barnes's syndrome? Would that make a difference?"

Now I hesitated. But I said, "No. We all suffer from that occasionally."

"Just checking you for exceptions. My, but you're so resolute! You wouldn't let your wife be touched even by an impotent man?"

He was chiding me.

"Something tells me you're not impotent."

"But if I was?"

For a million dollars? Maybe I would. I had to be honest. Maybe I would. Finally, he had me submitting to doubt, visibly so, judging from his pleased reaction. Student that he was of human frailties, he could tell I was *thinking*, tallying in my mind the new odds, suddenly quite favorable.

The risk on my part had been significantly reduced, if he were indeed impotent, which I doubted. But arguing *exceptions* was the same as arguing price, and arguing either was a fall from the heights of righteousness.

Whether he was impotent or not was almost beside the point. The purpose was to get me thinking, doubting my absolutes. There were no absolutes, he was saying. There were no truths. Name the absolute, he was saying, name the truth—and I'll name the price. Let's see which prevails.

"Of course I'm not impotent," he said. "But maybe I am. Maybe I am. I'm paying you a million dollars to find out. You're a gambler, Mr. Kane! Why else are you in Atlantic City?"

Good question, I thought. I was in Atlantic City to win big money. But not like this. There had to be a way to win it clean. Or maybe there wasn't. Maybe this was the only way. To gain a million dollars you had to give up the equivalent, something just as valuable, or even more valuable.

"I saw your face at the blackjack table," Ibrahim continued. "That was the face of a loser, Mr. Kane. Am I right? Of course I'm right. You want to be rich! Everybody wants to be rich. I must tell you this—no man on earth would reject the offer I'm making you. One million dollars? That is money no man can refuse. It is almost like turning down *eternity*. It is almost like renouncing *para-*

dise. For all that what do I ask? One night." Now he paused for a theatrical afterthought—"And I may just be impotent."

That was his down-card. Offer your wife and he flips it over.

That was the gamble.

"Think of it as blackjack," he said. "Think of it as any game of chance."

One night. With a man who may be impotent. For a million dollars.

The unthinkable had become thinkable.

The next thing to say was this: And what if he is *not* impotent? It's only one night.

It's still a million dollars.

So it was done, the whittling of a man's absolutes.

Ibrahim was obviously a master at this. He had played this game before. Not necessarily for another man's wife, but for other prizes. Perhaps the game itself was the real delight. The prize could not equal the pleasures of negotiating, of finagling. The catch could not equal the exhilaration of the hunt. His joy was in watching the power of his money strip men and women of their vanities. In that sense he wanted *me*, my capitulation, as much as he wanted Joan.

When a man had so much money that no *thing* was beyond his reach, he had nothing left but to play for people. What begins as a solution to boredom leads to contempt, and Ibrahim's contempt for his fellow man was as wide as he was handsome.

Now, from an end table, Ibrahim drew a Cuban Monticristo cigar from a cedar-lined humidor and began a loving process. He sniffed the length of the cigar to inhale its fragrance, licked it to tighten the leaf and then dipped it in the cognac. He let it dry and then drew a V-cutter from his vest pocket and made a perfect V-incision. He struck a wooden stick match along the matchbox and waited ten seconds for the top layer of sulfur to burn off. He lit up by rotating the cigar in his mouth, distributing the flame evenly along the length, never letting the flame actually touch the leaf. He took a short draw and was in business.

"I'm sorry," he said, extending the humidor. "Care for one? Cuban."

"Thank you, but I would not do it justice."

"Maybe so," he said.

If this man had one shortcoming, I thought, it was underestimating his opponent. That could be used against him. I did not know how. But somehow. Let him be almighty, I thought, and let me be meek. Then I'd surprise him. Somehow surprise him.

"For past favors," he said, "I owe you more than a cigar. The other day you really were good luck to me, as you could see for yourself. I did promise to make it worth your while." He drew a bulky white envelope from inside his jacket and placed it atop the humidor. "That's yours," he said.

It was, it was mine! Those were wages, the ten thousand dollars I figured were in there, in that envelope, an arm's length away. That money was mine as surely as my paycheck. An oral agreement had been made. I had fulfilled my end. Now it was his turn.

Yet how could I take the money?

And damn it, I needed the money. How I needed that money!

Just lean over and take it, I thought. It is yours. This is not part of that other deal. This is separate. This is *clean*. This is kosher. This is blessed. This is not tainted. This is *earned* money. This is *good* money. This is *honest* money.

But it was also a test, a trap, a snare, a trick to gather me in. Take this money, I thought, and you've submitted. Had he seen this from the start and saved it for now?

If so, he had this calculated even more than I had imagined. Now I understood why he had withheld payment at the blackjack table. For this moment. Then, it would have been wasted—valueless as negotiating power. Now it was useful. He had set me up by degrees. He had everything figured. Down to knowing that I would show up here instead of Joan. He had her figured, too. He knew she'd tell me. Was there anything he didn't know?

"Take it," he said. "It's yours."

"No," I said, "it's yours. What's yours is yours. What's mine is mine."

He got the point, but I had won nothing. As perfectly as he had this planned, surely he had foreseen this rejection. I was up against cunning, and defeatism set in. The thing about a loser is this: he expects to lose. Oh, but I was a winner.

"Don't you feel well?" he said.

"I'm fine."

"You look pale. I have a physician in the other room. You look very pale."

I knew the game. It was a typical gambler's ploy to

diminish and intimidate, and yet it was true that I felt clammy and strange in my clothes and irritated about the air conditioning. There was none of it here in Ibrahim's rooms, perhaps because of some religious prohibition against manufactured air. But I was beginning to suffocate.

Of course, being a son of desert nomads he was accustomed to heat.

Now I felt myself grow weak and unable to breathe, and this sensation, when I suspected each breath to be my last, was accompanied by chills and blurred vision and the shakes.

Our family doctor had found nothing physical but had diagnosed my occasional condition as a relatively mild case of Fear of People Syndrome, the sort that afflicted Howard Hughes, Greta Garbo and J. D. Salinger, meaning that I was in good company.

But it came upon me rarely, this dread of people, and this was one of those rare times—Ibrahim now looming as the giants of Canaan and me, yes, the grasshopper.

I was trembling and tried to keep it hidden from him, but he was smiling and I thought, *I must get out*.

I thought back to the time of the World's Fair in New York. I worked the night shift, so in the mornings I made my way up the ramp alone and down they came from the elevated subways, the tourists by the thousands, blind to my efforts to find a path against this surge of humanity. I felt so utterly small and inconsequential and even separate and apart from the human race.

Exactly as now.

Don't die, I thought. Not now. Save it for later.

I called on my reserves and somehow managed to rise. I staggered to the door, which kept changing places. But I found it and left Ibrahim sitting there, following me with those eyes of Esau-the-Hunter.

CHAPTER
11

THE ELEVATOR dropped me to the slot machine graveyard. There was no exit from there, except to the casino, so I walked in. I was in the mood anyhow.

Lights flashed in my face, blinking neons above the progressive slot machines circling jackpot figures of $25,000, $50,000, $100,000, $250,000—and even one million dollars!

Otherwise it was dark. It was always nighttime in the casino, to make people forget the outdoors. There were no clocks, to make people forget time. They even hid the water fountains, the bathrooms and the exits. This, ladies and gentlemen—they tried to tell you—this is the entire world! Thou shalt have no other worlds before you.

Right now that was fine with me. I needed to forget time and place and myself.

I made the rounds. End to end, the tables were brimming with people. Blackjack, baccarat, craps, roulette, Big Wheel, the people sat before these altars as intense as in prayer. Here, answer to prayer came swiftly, though not always affirmatively, with each turn of a card and each roll of the dice. Here it was decided who shall become rich and who shall remain poor. Mercy and punishment were meted out. This was heaven and this was hell.

I caught the flow of the place and felt its magic, its intoxicating pull. I drifted from aisle to aisle. There was nothing else like this—money! The religion of money. Chance—the worship of chance.

I saw a man place hundred-dollar chips on each of the thirty-eight numbers of the roulette table—each number but one. That was the number that came up. He wanted to protest. You could see the cry in his face. But there was no one to argue with. The ball and wheel were the final authority, the last word.

I saw a man at the craps table whispering to the dice cupped in his hand and then yelling after them when he tossed them out. This should be strange, I thought, whispering to dice, *yelling* at dice. But it wasn't. Not at this temple, where nothing was strange, nothing was wrong. Even greed was right.

But greed was the wrong word. No, the frenzy spoke of something deeper, a final grasp at life before the coming of death. *Make it happen for me*, was the entreaty—before I die.

Those middle-aged women by the slots—where did they get such mean faces? How did they get to look so much alike? These were the disdained bus people, the day-trippers. They came from all over, but they were row-house people, nothing about them to suggest open spaces or freedom of any sort. They had the downcast expressions of people who had aged harshly, trapped by trivial certainties. These were the wives of salaried men, their lives fixed to incomes rather than to dreams.

They were the Americans you never saw and never would have seen but for the casinos. The casinos lured them from their hiding places. By the multitudes they came, purposeful and fierce, to claim their share of the American jackpot. With each pull of the handle they declared, "Gimme, gimme. It's *mine*."

I was no different. Along with them I said, "Gimme. I want a better life. I'm owed something better."

That big bald fat man by the craps table, black hundred-dollar chips rolling in his hands, fat black cigar rolling in his mouth—why should he have it so good?

No, envy wasn't the problem. Neither was greed. Justice was what I sought. That's what we were all after. Life was unfair, damn it, except for the rich. So the purpose was to make life fair. That's what this was all about.

Joan was not in the room when I got back. I dialed the front desk to find out the time—I never carried a watch—and was told it was 7:30. I had told Joan I'd be back from Ibrahim's no later than 6:30. So, I thought, she must be having dinner by herself. Or maybe not.

I worked myself up into a panic. She could be anywhere, I thought, including Ibrahim's. No, impossible. Yes, he had threatened to make her the offer if I didn't, but this was too soon—and would she have gone running anyway? Let's not get ridiculous.

Rather than go hunting her down I decided to stay put. I clicked on the TV for company and it did not help. I missed her. She so filled the empty dimensions of my life that without her I was nothing.

Out in public places, when she was not with me, my head always turned at the sight of a golden crown of hair. When I was alone I still talked to her. I had allowed her to become everything, and no man should ever let any woman do that to him.

Maybe, I thought, she somehow knew about my conversation with Ibrahim! If so, she'd rightfully be furious. So maybe she had packed up and left. I checked the closet. Everything was there—Gucci luggage, Aigner sandals, Charles Jourdan pumps, Nipon wrap dress and all manner of other linen skirts and dresses, pants, jump suits and whatever else she had salvaged from her first marriage.

The book she'd been reading, Erich Maria Remarque's *Arch of Triumph*, was on the bed. She was near the end. I'd read it first and we had already been discussing it, especially the idea that women ruled the world of love. Love was a woman's domain, according to Remarque. Man? He was a stranger in a strange land.

Joan thought the notion stupid. Another thing to blame on women.

In the Remarque book, the heroine loved the hero but saw nothing wrong in having other men. Personally, said Joan, that sort of arrangement was not for her—but she could understand it. Yes, she could see how a woman could love one man and still have others. Don't men do the same?

With men it's different, I had said.

Oh! The old double standard! Men can but women can't!

Sometimes I provoked her just to watch her arch up into a full princess.

So where was she?

I should have socked him, I now thought. But that would have gained nothing. He probably had a plan against that, too. The offer would still have been good; and with that offer, take it or leave it, sock him or don't sock him, he had me. How perfectly he had me.

Joan arrived close to eight o'clock.

"Hi," she said.

"Hi."

"Where were you all this time? Did you slay the dragon?"

"Where were *you?*"

"I had dinner. By myself, since you weren't around. I played some slots, finally."

"You?"

"Just to kill time."

"Did you win?"

"Yes—but not the million-dollar jackpot."

"Maybe you did."

"What?"

I told her everything.

She fell back on the bed in a fit of exultation. "Oh God," she said. "Oh God! Did you say no at least?"

I paused.

"Of course."

"You don't seem sure."

"Of course I'm sure."

"So why did you hesitate? If you hesitated now you must have hesitated then."

"I did not hesitate."

Now we were silent, waiting for the other to say something—something smart, funny, wise, profound or whatever the occasion demanded. But what was the occasion? Who was the injured party? *Was* there an injured party?

Joan did not seem to think so. She was now in one of those Main Line moods that I never could figure out, half serious, half mocking, all female. It was impossible to take her at her word when she was like this, and impossible not to.

The playful look was now all over her happy face.

"The offer does sound good," she said.

"Stop it, Joan."

"Hmm. A million dollars for my body. Did you check the Guinness Book of World Records?"

"No, but I'm sure this is the top price ever."

"Are you impressed?"

"Oh, I'm very impressed, Joan."

"Well, now we both know what I'm worth. Not bad, don't you think?"

"What are you getting at, Joan?"

"Me? I'm getting at nothing, sweetheart. What are you getting at?"

Sweetheart was a word she used only when she meant to be tactless.

"Let's not go round on this," I said.

"Exactly."

"Exactly what?"

"I'm game, Josh. Exactly that."

"This is nothing to tease about, Joan."

"I'm not teasing."

"You better believe you are."

"Oh, but I'm not. I'd be doing it for you, Josh. I'm happy with my life. You're miserable. Just think. No more work. No more buses, subways. We'd be able to leave Philadelphia, which you hate. Buy a home, buy a car. Two cars. Three cars. Pay for your kids' college. Travel. Stay in Israel, which you love, for a year, two, three or however long you like. Of course, you being so religious and all, you'd give ten percent to charity. Who knows? *Your* money could find the cure for cancer. All that for one night with me. Doesn't sound like much of a sacrifice."

"In case I didn't make it clear, we're talking about your body."

"You made it very clear. My body. Not my heart. Not my mind. Not my soul. Those you'll always have. My body you'll lose for a night. Big whoop. What's a body?"

"Very big whoop."

"A million dollars, Josh. The jackpot, Josh."

"Can you believe we're having this conversation?"

"I can," she said. "Somehow I expected *something* like this to happen. You've always wanted to be rich. You've prayed for it and now your prayers have been answered, in a cruel sort of way, of course. But then, you expect your God to be cruel, so He is. Yes, there's a price. There's always a price. But you're not giving up that much. What's sex? Another bodily function."

"That's almost word for word what *he* said. You two do have much in common."

"Oh don't make this a romance, Josh. This isn't love. This is money."

"And as you say, first take the money, then be proud."

"No," said Joan. "First you have to *earn* the money."

That was a jab to the heart, and she knew it, as surely as she knew what *earn* meant in this discussion.

"How practical you are," I said.

"That's what I am, practical."

Only the other night she loved me more than anything. Nothing could come between us. She'd still say the same thing now. But now—now *practical* was the word.

"Yes," I said, "practical you are."

"Yes, and practical you're not."

"So he wins. The Arab wins."

"No, we win."

"He'll touch you."

"I'll survive."

"He'll *penetrate* you."

"You said he might be impotent."

"I don't believe that for a second."

"So he'll penetrate me. I'll shut my eyes and think of the million dollars."

"Joan, this makes you a whore!"

"So?"

"That doesn't bother you?"

"No. Anyway, isn't that the gospel according to Sy? We're all whores."

"You mean he's right?"

"Of course he's right."

"I don't understand women."

"I don't understand men. You want me to go ahead with this. I know you do."

"I do not."

"Yes you do. It shows."

"Where?"

"Everywhere."

"Something I said?"

"No, it's what you're not saying."

"What am I not saying?"

"Never mind."

"Is there a magic word?"

"For what?"

"To persuade you that I want no part of this thing. Is there a magic word to kill this ugliness between us now?"

"No, it's too late for magic words. I have no choice. *We* have no choice. We have to go ahead with this. You do see that, of course. Our lives are already changed. Every time a bill comes along that we can't pay, or your boss gives you a hard time, or the car breaks down, or the dishwasher goes on the blink—we'll think of that million dollars. That's how big this thing is. No, we can't go back. It's too late. Rejecting the offer would tear us apart more than accepting it. The freedom, Josh! You're being released from bondage. You won't have to write phony speeches for phony big shots anymore. You sell out every day. Now it's my turn and I'm willing. Freedom, Josh. Freedom to say yes when you mean yes, freedom to say no when you mean no. It's yours now."

I remembered what Ibrahim had said about turning

down eternity, renouncing paradise. A million dollars could buy more than just material things. In fact, that was the lesser benefit. The big gain was the freedom, all right, the freedom a man lost when he became a husband, a father, a worker. From the time he woke up in the morning to the time he went to bed at night, he had to answer to somebody. I'd always said that everybody owns a piece of a man. Well, that was only true of the poor man and the middle-class man. A rich man owned himself. What was that like, I often wondered—to own the rights to your beliefs and inclinations? To say what you want to say, do what you want to do? Joan was so right. Say yes when you mean yes, no when you mean no—how many men could do that? Very few.

"Only this goes against everything we believe in," I said. "Where do we go from here?"

"You mean after the deed? We'll live as always. Only with more money."

Practical. Logical. Too practical. Too logical.

Yes, the *deed*. What about the deed?

"I'll always know you had been with another man."

"You already know. I was married before, remember? So were you."

"We weren't married then, not to each other."

"No, but we've had sex with other people. That diminishes nothing between us."

"But that was before. This is now."

"So pretend it's before."

Juggle time, as the mystics do. The past, the present, the future were not necessarily in that order. The big mind was not fixed to the earthly procession of time. The big mind was at liberty to turn the future into the past. So who said I had a big mind?

"Nothing will change, Josh. You'll forget."

"Suppose *you* won't forget?"

"Oh, he'll be that great? Josh, women don't fall in love over sex. Never."

I was learning. Suddenly lovemaking was a trifle. A bodily function. Unless, of course, it was between people in love, and Joan and I were in love. So between us it counted. With Ibrahim it would not count. At least that was the pitch.

She was right about this: our lives were already changed. Accepting the offer might destroy us. But rejecting the offer would surely destroy us. That million dollars would always be there, if not in our hands, then in our minds—and that would be worse.

Women don't fall in love over sex?

"How many times have you had sex?" Joan asked. "With me, your ex and other women?"

"I don't know. I don't keep the books."

"Can you remember one performance from another?"

I couldn't.

"You can't because sex is simply not that special. It's like smoking."

"Smoking?"

"Ask a smoker if he can remember one cigarette from another."

"If it's so ordinary, why is Ibrahim willing to pay a million dollars for you?"

"Oh—temptation is something else. Temptation is something else."

Again she was right. This was beginning to baffle me. Everybody was right. Somebody had to be wrong.

As for Joan, I could not get the measure of her sincerity. Surely, I thought, she was playing me, testing me, judging me. The truth was there, behind the smile she kept flaring on and off. But I did not know what it was, the truth. I did not know the truth about Joan. Maybe there was no truth, about her, about me, about anybody. Maybe there was no such thing as a steadfast heart.

Temptation was something else all right. But perhaps we were talking about another sort of temptation. Not Ibrahim's, but hers. She was, after all, the girl who believed in trying everything once, and what a once this would be!

The lack of outrage on her part taunted me. She seemed too willing. No doubts, no protests, no inhibitions, no indignation from this lady who so believed in the sanctity of the female self. No revulsion from this lady who hated it when people near her coughed, sneezed, scratched or only cleared their throats.

No fealty from this lady who once said she'd kill me if she caught me with another woman. Nothing but acquiescence and curiosity and something approaching delight.

She should be horrified, I thought, and yet she isn't. Her body, man! Never mind this business about heart, mind and soul. It's supposed to be a package deal, this. What *do* they dream of at night in their pink bedrooms on the Main Line?

As for me, I was feeling the sting of betrayal. But who was the betrayer? I was as guilty as Joan.

You want me to go ahead with this, she had said.

This could not be true. Although, yes, I did compromise myself five days out of every week and so you figure what's *one night?*—for the lady. This one's on her. For the big payoff. Yes, her turn.

Think of the rewards! This payday was unto everlasting.

So is it right? No.

But is it wrong?

Can something be right *and* wrong, and is there such a thing as a small sin?

Is one night of adultery the same as a lifetime of it, and is it okay if the husband consents?

Never.

Absolutely never.

"Actually, it's not prostitution," she now said.

"Actually, it is."

"No, just the opposite. We get that one night over with and we're home free. The way we've been living, isn't that prostitution? Others dictating to you! *Using* you. Isn't that the very definition of being a prostitute? If anything, we'd be reversing the prostitution going on every day in our lives."

"That's called rationalizing."

"Or reality."

Ask yourself this question, I thought. The test of tests. Suppose your mother, your holy mother, had been offered this same indecent proposal? What would you have wanted her to do? Turn it down, of course!

♠   127   ♠

Oh, really?

Remember her . . . rushing to turn off the radio before the live-in landlord came home, and his finding out about it, clever and cunning Mr. Sherchock, by placing his hand atop the radio—and behold! It was warm.

Such wisdom all of a sudden from a man who owned a beauty shop on Park Avenue, a bachelor who paraded his women for us and left cigar ashes on his bureau to test Mother's efficiency. Nothing better to do with his time but think of such things, think of placing his hand on the radio—and *it was warm!*

The horror on her face, this woman who in the Old Country had had three housemaids waiting on her.

The reprimand: "Didn't I tell you, Mrs. Kane? Didn't I warn you? No radio. I have no money to burn on electricity. I better not catch you doing this ever again."

Remember her gift for liveliness, her flair for joy. Then that day her shoulders sagged and her mouth fell and the bounce left her step and the light departed from her eyes and even her voice, as from a distant world.

All of this forever, till the end of her days, for she had seen the truth in a flash, and not on a day when Father came home with bad news but *good* news. He'd found a new partner and was starting a new business and in a year, *you'll see, we'll be back dancing with the Bronfmans.*

On this day she knew. *It would never get better.*

For twenty more years nothing ever stirred her again. She went through the motions. Life was something she had already done and the rest of it was just waiting to die. Even her son's coming home the war hero was as nothing to her. Her husband, let him celebrate, but to her a hero was a man who made money.

Poverty, never mind the want, but the *degradation*, this was the most dreadful thing.

Now . . . turn back to that moment of her revelation, and now make that offer.

Accept or reject?

Talking about a life, a one and only life.

Reject, of course. This can never be right. And yet . . .

. . . does a person have the right to choose misery? Given the *other* choice, meaning a million dollars in exchange of a night?

Yes, *choose the good so that you may live*. But suppose it's the bad that lets you live?

Define misery. Physical hardship, that's one thing, and almost anything may be excused for the sake of easement. But poverty—or the perception of poverty—is that suffering?

CHAPTER
12

WE TOOK that question for a walk. Joan now suggested we stroll the Boardwalk to lift this weight from us, and on first stepping out we felt restored by the crowds moving from one casino to another, the sounds of laughter and couples walking arm in arm. For a moment we stopped by the pavilion in front of the Tropicana and listened to the oompah band and watched a man doing flips and turns on roller skates atop a picnic table . . . reminding me of such spectacles on Mount Royal in Montreal, a man exactly like this being introduced as "direct from the United sssssssssssssssssss . . . Cigar Company . . ."

We stopped in Atlantic Books. The latest Philip Roth was out in paperback. As she picked up her copy I heard two women, both minimum-wage employees, talking of a nearby novelty shop. One said to the other:

"Just do it. It'll make the day go by faster."

What a way to live!

Make the day go by faster.

So it was like this for just about everybody. There were levels and degrees, but no person was able to deny another's sense of affliction. This *was* suffering.

Outside, I asked Joan, "Who said, 'We all lead lives of quiet desperation'?"

She said, "Thoreau."

"Walden?"

"Yup. 'The mass of men lead lives of quiet desperation. What is called resignation is confirmed desperation. A stereotyped but unconscious despair is concealed even under what are called the games and amusements of mankind.' "

Of course she knew the quote, Joan being Joan.

She said, "Yes, Josh. The secret's out. Thoreau knew it ahead of you."

"Do you agree with him?"

"Oh I don't know. I don't know. No, I don't think so. I've seen too many happy people."

"So have I. For an hour. A day. Maybe even a week. But day after day?"

"Oh yes," she said. "Day after day. My sister Sunny . . ."

"All right, she's sunny."

"Yes she is, and there are more where she came from."

"But suppose he's right . . ."

"Of course there are plenty of miserable people . . ."

"And suppose Ibrahim's offer went to one of them?"

She thought this over. "They'd take it," she said. "First, if you put it on a hypothetical level, sure they'd say no. That's reflex. *Who me? Never.* But put the power of real money behind the question and the answer is yes. Yes."

"So that's us," I said.

"That's us."

"Even though we're not miserable."

"That's a state of mind. Your state."

"My state."

"Yes. You're obsessed with money."

"But I'm not miserable."

"A person who doesn't have what he wants, what's that?"

"So I am miserable."

"No. Unhappy. You're unhappy and frustrated and that's why this makes sense."

"That's the only reason."

"That's the only reason," she said.

"You don't mind . . . being broke . . . driving around in that car . . ."

"I do mind. But so what? We're not alone."

"You can take it, right?"

"I can. But you can't. That's why I'm game."

I resisted saying *maybe too game.*

"You never wondered if I'd ever get us . . . comfortable?"

"No," she said. "I have confidence in you. You have talent. People are bound to realize your worth."

So much like my mother. The same cheerfulness and always so sure about the future. Just like my mother, and just like my mother Joan would wake up one day and see it all before her. Futility.

Was this the Joan I was making? The same woman my father had made of his wife?

In that case, Joan was right. It made sense. There was nothing to do but accept.

No way.

I did agree on this: I had talent. People were bound to recognize my worth. Oh sure.

But suppose this happened only after you were good and dead? After all, most people lived and died just like this.

I said, "The way we're talking, it's like a farewell."

As unexpected as an ambush, she stopped, turned and pulled me into a powerful embrace, planting wet kisses all over my face. "Never. Never never never. Nothing changes. Nothing. You're my husband and lover forever."

This made it all the more like a farewell.

We passed Convention Hall, which soon would be jumping for the Miss America Pageant, and then we caught a tram by leaping up while it was still moving. Joan was absolutely delighted by this cheap thrill.

We sat closely together.

"We don't do this often enough," she said, waving back to the people on foot.

Down on the beach a muscle-man in swim trunks was standing on his hands, and the lady next to Joan said, "There he is. He does it every night. That's all he does. I wonder if he's crazy."

Even now, in the dark, the locals were walking their dogs, the dogs skipping along the water's edge; and on the sands, couples, silhouetted and isolated against the expanse of the sea, were doing what was private.

In the pavilions and on the benches along the Boardwalk railing the elderly were gathered and seated, and some were not so old. There was talking and gesturing and whispering and laughter, clusters of people from all over, all over the world, accents and dialects and languages of all sorts, even English.

After a drought of some thirty years, Atlantic City was again the place to be. The Boardwalk, slowly coming back, was again the place to be seen.

I watched her from the corner of my eye. She was positively happy now . . . forgetting that offer from Ibrahim that had us in turmoil. She was exultant, smiling and laughing and making small talk with the other passengers on the tram. As much as she tried to be plain and ordinary and simple there was something about it, like a queen come down to mix with her subjects. She was wearing a white shawl and around her shoulders it was draped as a royal vestment. This lady had been to the *Riviera!* How could she get a kick out of this?

She had been in private planes, sports cars, speedboats, yet there was something so solid about her. She had once said, "I'm really a Jewish mother at heart. Oy vey."

To test this I took her to the Orthodox synagogue on Castor for the high holy days, and she was *appalled.*

"Oh it was beautiful," she had said. "The cantor and all the men in white. Such beautiful melodies and the Torah scrolls with their glittering crowns. Too bad I couldn't see or hear most of it because they *keep their women in the back.* Now why is that, Josh?"

"Because . . . Joan, it's too involved."

"In the back?"

"Talk to Gloria Steinem."

"In the back?"

"Trust me, Jewish women are more equal than men."

"I'll go wherever you want, Josh, really I will, but not second-class."

"Women don't have to go to synagogue anyway."

"But I want to go. Next time we'll go Reform again. It's so much like church. Why?"

"Why what?"

"Why don't women have to go to synagogue?"

"Because their prayers are already answered, just by being women."

"That is beautiful. No, I mean it. That's beautiful. But one day I'll talk to God about this business of keeping women hidden away in the back. She should know about this."

Now the tram passed Bally's Park Place and the Claridge and the Sands and we rode all the way to Showboat, where we got off. "Shall we go in?" said Joan.

"No," I said.

"You don't want to play?"

"No."

"You've never tried it here."

"They're all the same."

"This doesn't sound like my Josh."

Snap out of it, I thought. This is a great night. There really isn't much more.

She pulled me indoors and said, "All right, I'm going to play."

Which did not sound like my Joan.

"What?" I asked.

"Something."

"Look out, Showboat!"

She followed the crowds and found that the big action was by the video poker machines, the hottest games in town. Here, unlike most other slots—here you had choices and could make decisions.

"Do you even know how to play poker?" I said.

"Josh, see, you *don't* know me. Of course I know the rules of poker, silly boy. Played it in college."

"Strip poker?"

"Maybe once," she said. Our Lady of Once.

Mostly women, but a good number of men, were working the machines, tapping the buttons.

"Hold this machine," she said—the only one available amid the crush of players.

She got change at a Change Booth and came back with a roll of forty quarters. She was excited.

She put in a quarter at a time.

"Hon," said a lady, "a quarter at a time gets you nothing. You got to put in all five quarters."

"Thanks," said Joan, but continued slipping in a quarter per play.

"I know this machine," said the lady. "It can get hot."

Sure enough it did. Four of the cards were diamonds, and in this order: ten, jack, queen, king. She needed an ace of diamonds for the jackpot. "Josh," she said, "do you see this?"

"Yes," I said, but she only had a quarter going, and she'd only get back some more quarters, instead of a thousand dollars had she put in all five, as the lady said.

Joan held the four good cards, pressed Draw, and up came the ace of diamonds. *Royal flush*.

She yelped, "Josh!"

The machine rang up a few credits.

"You just *lost* a thousand dollars," said the lady.

Joan didn't mind. She'd gotten herself a royal flush!

I didn't mind, either. So what? A thousand dollars.

I mean so what? A thousand dollars.

We blew a thousand dollars.

Who needs a thousand dollars?

I was sweating. What happened to the air conditioning? Don't they air condition these places anymore? I thought of that movie, *Hole in the Head* or something, with Frank Sinatra playing the poor shiftless guy against the big shot Keenan Wynn. They're pals from way back, Sinatra trying to pass himself off as a successful guy himself. They're at the racetrack, both with big bets on the same horse, Sinatra having sunk all his money on this horse. The horses are off and running. Here's Sinatra up on his toes, sweating and hollering, and there's Wynn, seated and calm because it's just another bet for him, watching Sinatra, seeing the desperation, the loser in him.

In an instant, the loser had given himself away.

So don't go giving yourself away, I thought, and when we left the casino I tried to be cheerful.

"I got a royal flush," she said.

"You sure did."

"Hope I don't get hooked. *That was fun*."

"Sure was."

No mention of the thousand dollars. She did not see things that way.

We walked back, and near Bally's Park Place police had a black man down on the ground. Bystanders said he had snatched a purse. The black man, held tight to the boards by five officers, was saying, "It wasn't me. Let me go."

They had him pinned in police hold number two.

I turned to Joan. "Do something?" I said.

"There's nothing to do," she admitted, but we sped up and hastened back to the Galaxy.

But before heading back to our room, a thought suddenly depressing, we strolled over to the Boardwalk railing and gazed out at the ocean. We stood there for some time and said nothing, and I knew her mind was working—she kept shooting me side glances, occasionally sighing and smiling and now and then gently touching my face.

One of the rolling-chair boys shouted out, "Give the lady a ride!"

I waved back.

Before he took off again he said, "Beautiful lady like that!"

Then it became so quiet again, as if everybody had left. She resumed her study of the ocean, following the waves lapping in gently, and she turned to me in great determination to say something monumental—staring firmly into my eyes and pressing her hand against my chest. But no words came. She *had* said something monumental, but she kept it to herself. Then she turned from me to face the ocean again.

I felt that something great and deep, and wonderful and awful, had just passed between us, only I didn't know what it was, exactly, except for this powerful impact of the unsaid.

Now she said, "My father . . . for a time I thought all men were like my father. He was, and he is, a brutal man. Not physically. Never touched me or my mother or my sister, but that made him no less brutal.

"He had wanted boys, and we were girls, and he never took us anyplace and he seldom talked to us. He had no patience at all for girls, and I'm not so sure he'd have been different with boys.

"He actually *blamed* Mother for giving birth to girls, as though it were all her fault. She asked him, she said, 'Would you have been happier with no children at all?' He said yes. Yes! He even said that to my face, and Sunny bawled for a week.

"But it's a strange thing between daughters and their fathers. I remember when we went to see him off at the airport that one time, and when they started boarding I waited for him to turn and wave to me and—he didn't. I felt so *devastated*.

"I must have been about twelve and it made a terrific impression.

"I thought all men were like this . . . like my father. Oh I had a wonderful childhood in many ways. Of course we were wealthy, but when you grow up wealthy you don't know you're wealthy. I mean we passed all those slums when we had to go into Philadelphia—but that was just scenery.

"Father even said, 'These aren't real people. Think of them as *extras*.'

"I'm not kidding.

"Charles was the same way, and I'm sorry to bring his name up but he *was* my first husband. I mean he was and that's a fact and I thought I loved him. Because I was supposed to love him.

"He was a good man and he loved me but he was so . . . I mean he never exceeded himself. He never surprised me. I once bought him a book for his birthday—he only read those legal things, so I thought I'd buy him something literary, Updike I think it was—and he said, 'What would I want with this?'

"So I could see it happening. This was my father all over again.

"You've met my father. You were there when he said 'nothing is offensive.'

"Well Charles was more sensitive, but not by much.

"Then you came along . . . Josh, it was so different . . . so exciting.

"If you only knew how much I loved you, from the very beginning.

"You were so perfect. In your own quiet way, so dashing. You were shy and brash and confident and insecure and so masculine and so vulnerable and you had been around and seen things and done things and yet you were not spoiled or ruined by it all, and not even cynical, though you like to think of yourself as cynical. But you're not. No, Josh. You're open and available.

"I've been around, too, though not in the ways you

JACK ENGELHARD

have, all these things in Europe and then in Israel and the women you've tried not to tell me about—but I've heard. Some rake you were. I've told you I've only been with two men, Charles and you, and it's true. But my life really started when I met you. That's when the adventure began. *You* are my adventure.

"You're not a woman so you'll never understand, but take it from me, however liberated a woman is, she lives to please her man. It's as old as the caves and there are a million exceptions, but it is the rule.

"I'm a *woman*, Josh, and you know I fight for my rights—make all the fun you want about us whining about our disadvantages while sipping iced tea on the veranda of the country club.

"All right, I'm not wholly with them and I'm not wholly against them. I'm me, an individual, an irreplaceable soul as you say, and the point is this—I may fight it when I find myself getting too confined, too much *into* you, too much a part of you, but I am yours. *I want to please you.*

"I'm that old-fashioned.

"I mean even the sex we do . . . you must admit some of it is kinky. But it pleases you so it pleases me—and I love it! I never thought I would do all those things, but I do love it, Josh.

"But it's not only the sex. The sex is even the least of it. It's everything else. The books you read, the thoughts you think, the feelings you feel—I want all of that for me.

"I wish I had been there with you in France, and on those sidewalks in Montreal, and I even wish I could have been there with you in battle. No, I'll never under-

♠   142   ♠

stand you and you'll never understand me—but that's the fun.

"I even have dreams of being a nurse and saving your life and falling in love. It's rare, isn't it, to have fantasies about the man you already have!

"You have to know all this, Josh, no matter what happens. And we know things are happening and we're scared and we have every right to be because to use that word—it's awesome, this thing. It's awesome.

"But you have to know that even when I get *modern* on you, and liberated, and rebellious, and remain a shiksa, deep inside I'm your Sarah, your Rebecca, your Rachel, your Leah. Now let's go inside."

Now in our room, reality was back. Ibrahim and his offer were alive and well and living in Atlantic City.

Time to go.

She took her shower and got into her night things, and I said, "I'm ready."

"You are?"

"To go home."

"Our vacation isn't over," she said.

"For me it is."

"Isn't this running away?"

"Yes it is."

"You can't run from this, Josh."

"Watch me."

"You're a fighter, Josh."

"So I'm fighting."

"By running away?"

"Strategic retreat."

"You're a war hero. You have all those medals from Israel."

"I can face an Arab with a rifle. How do I stand up to an Arab with a million dollars?"

We sat down on the bed. Now we were weary. Exhaustion overtook us both at the same time. As if by signal we knew we had come to the end, for now. Joan's face, usually shaded by high crimson, was now chalk white.

"So what do we do?" she asked.

"Forget," I said. "We forget this whole thing."

"Whatever you say."

"I still think we should go home."

"Whatever you want. I love you, Josh."

"I love you, Joan."

I decided against joining her in bed. Instead I went down to the casino to play my game. Blackjack.

I won $180. Once upon a time that would have been a fortune. I'd have sped up to Joan to report the wonderful news. But now . . . what was $180? Compared to, say, a thousand.

Compared to, say, a *million?*

We left Atlantic City the next morning.

CHAPTER
13

THE ALARM woke me at six. Monday morning, this was, in Philadelphia. Atlantic City was over. Philadelphia had begun. Joan was slumbering beside me. She still had a week to go on her vacation. My time was up. The alarm said so.

"I hate Philadelphia," I said as I pulled myself out of bed.

"You're waking me," Joan murmured into her pillow. "Please be more quiet."

So I leaned over and whispered in her ear. "I hate Philadelphia. Have I told you lately how much?"

"Yes."

"You'll never know how much."

"I know. I know. Shh."

What shall I wear today? I wondered. Me and my wardrobe of two and a half suits. I did a lot of mixing and matching. I'll mix and match again today, I thought. No, I'll wear the blue suit. Should wear a suit on my return.

Should wear a suit always, of course, this being the wonderful world of business. Public relations no less. Not to mention that this was the age when we were all supposed to look as if we'd been processed instead of born.

But as often as not I wore jeans to the office and that upset the people, one vice president in particular. Word got back to me—from Myer Lipson—that this vice president had said, "The way Josh dresses you can tell he's not serious about his job."

Serious? I should be serious about this job? Brain surgery, that's serious! This was business. Didn't anybody see the joke? Was I the only one who knew what was beneath the bottom line?

The way they talked market and profit you'd think they were going to live forever. If anything, these business people died sooner than most. They had short life spans and, as far as I could tell, they left everything behind, even their markets and profits.

Blue suit, I said to myself. I'll wear the blue suit. I checked the armoire drawers.

"I only have one pair of shorts left," I said.

"I have to do a wash."

"Only one pair of socks."

"So? Wear them."

"But they're brown. I was going to wear my blue suit today."

"So wear your brown suit."

"No shirts to go with the brown suit."

"The white shirt," she said.

"The blood stain is still on the collar."

"It's just a speck. It's almost out. You should get the soles fixed on your shoes. Need heels, too."

"Tomorrow."

I tottered to the bathroom, urinated, showered and cut myself shaving in the same spot as always, right by the Adam's apple. I ruined more shirts that way. Damn, that got me mad.

"Why are you swearing?"

"Cut myself shaving. I hate Philadelphia."

I got dressed in the blue suit and brown socks. Who looks at socks anyway? I went down for the paper.

"Guess what?" I said. "No paper."

"Call."

"I don't have time to call. They keep you on hold for an hour. They play music while you wait. You call."

"When I get up."

"Can't get a decent paperboy these days. I hate Philadelphia."

I had some corn flakes and a cup of hot tea.

"Bye," I said.

"Have a nice day."

"Too late."

I walked up to the bus stop on Old Bustleton. I passed neighbors getting into their cars. We didn't talk. We only talked in the wintertime when we were all out shoveling snow. In the summer we never talked.

Once I talked to a neighbor and a week later he installed an aluminum fence around his house. Then he bought a mad dog that went berserk any time I passed the property. I got the hint.

Now I waited for the bus. Please God, I prayed, let it be air conditioned and let there be a seat.

But no bus showed up. Are they on strike? I wondered. I hadn't been following the news. Somebody was always on strike. In this city they thought nothing of shutting down schools, highways, trains, garbage collection and even hospitals. This was a city that did not work.

The bus did come though, as ordered, air conditioned and with room to sit. Incredibly, I did not have the right change. For three years I'd been doing this routine—but today I forgot. The smallest I had was a ten.

"Exact change only," said the bus driver.

"You mean you won't give me change?"

"Exact change only."

I turned to the people on the bus. I said, "Can somebody here give me change for a ten?"

But I was talking to the dead. A bus full of dead people.

"All right," I said to the driver. "Will you take my ten?"

"Put it in the machine."

I had to slide the bill through a slot, face up. But I didn't. I tried to slide it through face down. The bus driver—all he had to do was tell me, remind me. But he just sat there and watched me. They don't tell you anything here in the City of Brotherly Love. They just watch you. Finally, I got it right.

These new buses were built for half-assed people. I squeezed in, in the back of the bus, between a middle-aged lady to my left and a well-dressed—for Philadelphia—man to my right. He was about thirty and there was nothing especially disgusting about him.

I took out a book from my briefcase to have cover in case it got crowded and some old lady tried to pity me out of my seat. I used to be a sucker for old ladies, but the Philadelphia variety were so mean-spirited that there was no choice but to be scornful of them.

As we moved along I did some sightseeing on Bustleton Avenue. Trash everywhere! Incredible. I should have been used to it by now, but I wasn't. I wondered, are the *brooms* on strike? The outdoor garbage containers had signs that said Help Keep Philadelphia Clean. Keep? This is clean? But yes, in Philadelphia filthy was clean.

The well-dressed man to my right let out a big juicy ball of spit.

"What?" I said.

He did not hear me. He was also dead.

What am I doing here!

In the winter they coughed in your face, sneezed, wheezed and snorted. You thought you were in a zoo. In the summer it wasn't so bad. But now I had me a spitter. That was something new.

I'd often said that the inhabitants should be removed from Philadelphia, and then the place ought to be bombed. Now I wasn't so sure, I mean about removing the inhabitants.

How, I wondered, did all the slobs of the world manage to collect in one place? How did they all find Philadelphia? Had there once been a convention where it was decided that this was the promised land for slobs?

This had been the city of the Declaration of Independence. Now it was the city of the *soft pretzel*. This was the city that went mad when Leonard Tose threatened to move the Eagles football team to Phoenix. Years earlier when the teachers went on strike nobody cared, certainly not as much.

Then, of course, there were the Mummers . . .

Now he spat again, a big fat juicy blob of spit.

"Hey," I said.

I gave him an elbow.

"Yo!" he said.

That was what they said here: "Yo!"

Yo, Angelo!

He spat again.

I thought, I paid ten dollars—*ten dollars!*—for this?

"Slob," I said.

Right, I thought, Slob City USA.

He spat again. There was now a puddle in front of us.

I gazed around for support, for an uprising. But no, they were still dead, the other passengers.

One more time, I thought, and I belt him in the mouth. For now, I merely tapped his hands. This was not *real* violence, but it was physical contact—and this was not like me, not at all, to hit people in peacetime. Only this was war.

"Yo!" said a voice from the front.

It was my friend the bus driver.

"What's going on back there?" he wanted to know.

"This guy's hitting me," the slob said.

"This guy's spitting," I said.

The bus driver stopped the bus—we were at Bustleton and Roosevelt—and walked back.

"All right," he said. "What's going on?"

"He's hitting me."

"He's spitting," I said, "on *your* bus."

"Aren't you the guy . . ."

"Yes," I said. "I'm the guy."

"I can order you off this bus."

"I paid ten dollars for this bus."

"Look. I don't want trouble."

"Tell this guy to stop spitting."

"No trouble, understand? Or I call the cops."

Most of the cops in Philadelphia were in jail anyway. The driver walked back to his seat and moved us out again.

"I have a condition," said the slob. He said it in such a confidential tone that I could not be angry at him anymore.

"What condition?"

"A condition."

"Everybody's got a condition," I said.

"Mine's special."

"Sorry to hear that," I said. "Sorry I hit you."

"You shouldn't go around hitting people."

"Usually I don't. You're the first."

Now the bus stopped at the terminal at Bridge and Pratt, and all the dead people got out and began a dash for the els, as the subways here are called. I got out with the rest of them and was met by heaps of debris and pigeons that flew straight for your face. They were also Philadelphians, the pigeons.

I got on a train and sat where somebody had just vomited and began the twenty-five-minute ride to Center City, a ride that took you past ten miles of rot on both sides. Nothing but windowless row houses, decaying factories, ravaged warehouses. Only the bars were still in business. There was graffiti on everything from top to bottom, from end to end, as a signature to surrender. This was a gasping city.

CHAPTER
14

THE OFFICE was on the seventh floor of a renovated building on Twelfth between Market and Chestnut. There had been a riot here a couple of weeks before I had left for vacation. Smashing and looting and nobody knew why. This wasn't the sixties. The mayor had said that it was just kids having fun.

Harvey Lint, the lobby newsstand man, now welcomed me back by offering me a free Hershey bar. He said his girl was still sick, out of commission as he put it, and that he still needed something temporary. Perhaps, Harvey said, from my office. But "quality." She had to be "quality."

"In Philadelphia," I said, "there is no quality."

Harvey laughed.

"Don't laugh," I said. "Have you ever seen a pretty face in this town?"

I took the elevator up and Helen Smith, the receptionist who had aged with the company, said, "Well well. Look who's back. How was Atlantic City?"

"Nice," I said. "Did I miss much?"

"Everything's the same, Josh. You know how it is."

I made straight for the bathroom to wash up, as always after the bus and subway ordeal. Just as I was finishing up a man from one of the other offices—where they sold communications systems—stepped out of a toilet cubicle and walked right out.

I thought, How come people don't wash their hands after taking a shit anymore? When did this begin? Lately I'd noticed that more and more. Maybe, I thought, they ought to teach this new generation less about computers and more about washing hands after a shit. Only that separated us from the four-legged animals anyway.

As I moved around the corner to my office, I said, "What am I doing here?"

Gloria Indoza, the secretary I shared with three other speechwriters, said, "You have a nine-thirty meeting in the conference room."

"Good to see you again, Gloria."

"I'm on a rush job."

Rush rush rush, as my father used to say. *America is rush rush rush.*

Myer Lipson walked into my office and sat down.

"Are you in on that meeting?"

"Hello, Myer. Did you miss me?"

"The place wasn't the same without you, Josh. Are you in on that meeting?"

"So I hear."

"They want you for the job."

"What job, Myer?"

"We got the account."

"What account?"

"You don't know?"

"I've been away, Myer."

Myer knew that, of course. Myer knew everything. But Myer had games to play. Straightforward was not his style, due to the fact that when God gave out ten measures of paranoia, Myer took nine. As for being insecure, he took the entire portion.

"We got the Friedrich account."

"They make soaps and detergents," I said, playing dumb.

"Plus everything else."

"The German company," I said.

"*Ya vol.*"

"Nazis."

"Now now Joshua, not all Germans are Nazis."

"They make soap? Out of what?"

Myer, of course, knew that they used to make soap out of Jews—the Nazis did. One could not be sure about this Friedrich. But one could suppose.

"Their CEO is going to be at the meeting," said Myer. "Flew in from West Berlin. Adolph Friedrich. Jules talked you up big, I understand. This Friedrich wants you and only you to write his speeches. This could be your big move, Josh."

Myer's envy was showing. He was terrified that I'd get to be vice president ahead of him. He was actually terrified of everything, Myer was. He so wanted to please and be loved. He was the perfect company man.

"It's all news to me," I said.

"I understand the account is worth a million dollars."

A million dollars again. Wherever I went, it seemed, a million dollars was sure to go.

"You're bound to get a raise," Myer said.

That also terrified him.

"If I accept," I said.

"You have to accept."

"I don't have to do anything."

"What makes you so cocky all of a sudden? Hit the jackpot in Atlantic City?"

"I'm a free man, Myer."

"That's the biggest joke of all. Who's free?"

"Myer," I said, "what are we doing here?"

"That's what I keep asking *you.*"

"Me, I'm just here to make a living. You're ambitious, Myer. You *care.*"

"I'm just like you, Josh. I don't care about anything."

"Myer, you care about everything!"

"I'm a family man."

"So, do the job, but don't care so much. Or you'll die by the time you're forty-two."

"I'm forty-three."

"So maybe you're dead already. Did you ever wonder about that?"

He would.

At nine-thirty we were all in the conference room, vice president after vice president, followed by me and then Myer. We were the only people here who were not vice presidents—including Jules Corson. He was the president.

He sat at the head of the long table and said: "Good morning. Thanks for being here." As if there were a choice. "Mr. Friedrich will be here shortly. This is a very big opportunity for us. The big one, in fact. Friedrich Corporation is a multibillion-dollar outfit. Their American subsidiary, headquartered in Milwaukee, is set for a major image blitz, if you know what I mean. Sales here are lagging. Morale is low. That's where we come in. Mr. Friedrich wants us to boost morale in this country, and we're to provide him the means to achieve his goals. This will be a total campaign—PR, publicity, collateral and all the rest. You know what I mean? First, though, we'll be writing his speeches so that he can pep up his key executives here. He'll be touring each plant. Joshua, you'll be heading the speechwriting team. Any questions?"

Of course not. Nobody ever had questions.

"Jules," I began.

"Josh," he said. "This is a great opportunity for you."

"I know, but does he speak English?"

Jules had a temper.

"Of course he speaks English."

"No accent?"

"Of course he has an accent. He's German."

"German accents can be . . ."

"Can be what?"

"Suggestive."

"Suggestive of what?"

"Harsh. Let's say harsh."

"In what way harsh?"

"In a militaristic way, Jules. How old is he?"

'I don't know, Josh. Why are you asking these questions?"

"You asked for questions," I said.

"Not *stupid* questions."

Myer was smiling. I could not see the smile, but I could feel it on my back.

"If I'm going to work with this man, shouldn't I know something about him?"

"Are you having a problem, Josh?"

"Maybe."

"What's the problem?"

"I'm not nuts about Germans."

"So? I'm not nuts about Japs, but I drive a Japanese car. Since when does nationality have anything to do with business?"

Jules had fought the Japanese in Burma. So he had once told me. Now he drove a Japanese car. He had made his peace. Now I had to make mine. For business.

Adolph Friedrich arrived with an assistant. He shook hands all around. Adolph was about thirty-eight. He was cheerful, friendly and an all-around pal. His face glowed from excessive good health. He had the complexion of a woman or even a baby. But his eyes were tiny and dull. There was something about his eyes.

"So," he said. "We have a nice family."

Why, I wondered, did his name have to be Adolph? Maybe if his name were Hans or Otto or Ludwig or Gustav I could stomach him. But Adolph was too much. Even for business.

His flunky—Otto, by the way—gave an hour's spiel on

the history of the company, how it got started in 1923 as a small soap producer in Hamburg and then expanded its product line and grew throughout Germany and then the world. Slides and a short film showed the whole thing, including the founders, Grandpa and Grandma Friedrich. Everything was here in this presentation except for one thing. There was no mention of the years 1939 to 1945. *What happened to those years?*

Strange, I thought, that those years should be omitted. Hadn't there been some sort of disturbance during that time? Even a war?

Following Otto's presentation, Adolph got up to make some closing remarks.

He said: "Today is the beginning of tomorrow. The future is where we are going. The opportunity is knocking for good and better business for us, for you, for everybody. Let us march forward to success. I am very gay."

This man—this man needs a speechwriter all right, I said to myself.

Jules Corson then got up and said, "Any questions?"

I raised my arm and Jules's face turned ugly. His lips snarled up as he said, "Yes, Josh."

"What I'd like to know . . ."

"Later, Josh. This meeting is over."

Myer smiled. He too was very gay.

Later, as threatened, I was in Jules's office. He had summoned me. He was on the phone, but that did not deter him from talking to me. In fact, Jules was incapable of holding one conversation at a time. He needed two.

"You need a vacation," he said.

"I just had one."

"Maybe something more permanent," he said.

"Jules, are you firing me?"

"I'd love to. But I can't. You're the best speechwriter I've got—which isn't saying much. But what the hell has gotten into you?"

"You know I'm not good with clients."

"But not like this. I've never seen you like this."

"What did I say?"

"It's what you were going to say."

"What was I going to say?"

"You tell me."

"I was merely going to ask how they made their soap."

"That could have killed the account. A million-dollar account."

"Jules, I can't write speeches for a Nazi."

"He's no Nazi, damn it, Josh!"

"His name is Adolph."

"That's unfair."

"I know, Jules. I'm not a fair person."

"He's too young to have been a Nazi."

"So his father was a Nazi. By the way, what happened between 1939 and 1945?"

"I don't know."

"Did you notice how those years just disappeared?"

"I don't care. We're not at war with Germany anymore."

"You're not. I am."

"I'm sorry to hear that, Josh. That will make it difficult for you to work on this account."

"So take me off."

"I can't. You're committed. It will do you good. Teach you forgiveness."

End of discussion. When I got back to my office, Myer was there, pretending to be thrilled for me.

"Myer, I'm not in the mood."

"What were you talking about in there with Jules?"

"About you, Myer. I talked him out of firing you again. This comes up every day, you know."

Myer knew I was kidding, of course—but he could never be absolutely sure.

"Did Jules make you a vice president?" he asked.

"Of course he did."

"Are you getting a raise?"

"Naturally—plus a bonus. There's no stopping me now, Myer."

"Jules really likes you."

"I know."

"He doesn't like me."

"That's for sure."

"Why doesn't he like me?" asked Myer.

"Because you try too hard."

"No I don't. I can be as easygoing as anybody."

I had already seen Myer be easygoing. At that too he tried hard.

"Don't be so gullible, Myer."

"Was he actually going to fire me?"

"No, he was actually going to fire *me*."

"You were a bit out of line, you know. But he likes that—your chutzpah. Let's have lunch."

We had lunch at the deli on Chestnut, the same group of five speechwriters. For none of us was this a profession of choice. No, it just *happened*. What was that line? *Life is what happens to you while you're making other plans.* Well, that was us.

Now I listened to the table talk. What had I missed during my absence? Not much. Amazing, I thought, how nobody had changed. Bob Porter still hated Republicans. Morris King still thought Israel was wrong about everything. As for Fred Manning, he still had the perfect filing system, which he himself had devised. If only Jules Corson would listen and adopt it for the whole company. But he refused. Fred was thinking of taking his perfect filing system elsewhere. Quitting. Myer? He was still worried about getting fired. Me, I had nothing much to say.

"What's the matter, Josh?" somebody asked. "You seem distant."

I should be less critical, I thought. Be more forbearing. These were my peers. I was no better. I was no worse. What's wrong with me? I asked myself. What do you want? I want this: something *different*. Doesn't even have to be *better*. Just *different*. Like what? There is nothing different. This is it, boy. You come in by bus, by subway, do some work, have lunch with the guys, work again, and again take the subway, the bus, get back, have dinner, watch TV, go to bed, and the next morning start all over again.

Doesn't anything change? Over and over and again and again it's the same thing. Thirty more years of this? I thought. Thirty more years of listening to Fred Manning talk about his filing system?

CHAPTER 15

NOW JOAN was nested in. Again the house belonged to her as a house could only belong to a woman. A man was only a visitor, even in his own home. She had made lunch plans for the week with Tilly, Bobbi and Sandi, all from the Main Line, and tennis plans for the weekend with Vera—also, of course, from the Main Line. She had been to the Acme, done three loads of wash, made an appointment with Roberto her hairstylist, and vacuumed and dusted the apartment. She was back in the center and life could revolve around her again.

Now—when I arrived home from work—she was in the kitchen preparing dinner. I had once told her that that was my second favorite moment, coming home and finding her in the kitchen. She was sure enough about herself to understand that as praise.

I took a quick shower and didn't bother to get dressed. I dashed for the kitchen and stripped her as she was mixing vegetable soup. Then I led her to the bedroom and we made love. This was a good one, with all the appropriate sighs, whimpers and then the big yell. I made love to her this day as a reaffirmation of ownership, because I knew that I did not own her.

I was finally beginning to realize that two people could never be one.

We showered together and then started dinner.

"How was it at work?" she asked.

"The same."

"That's good."

"It is?"

"Some things should be different. Some things should be the same."

"Well—not everything was the same." I told her how the bus had cost me ten dollars this morning, and how I had hit a guy on the bus.

"So you smacked him?" she said.

"He had it coming."

"That's not like you, Josh."

"I had a tough day, actually."

Now I told her about the Friedrich account.

"I should have known," she said. "You always get horny when something goes wrong."

"Passionate, Joan. I wish you wouldn't say *horny*. It's not a Main Line word."

"Please don't write my lines, Josh. *I* don't need a speechwriter."

Somehow you know it's coming, another quarrel, and you also know it can't be stopped. You want to stop it but you can't. It has its own power. It is fueled by who knows what pains and frustrations. The quarrel may have nothing to do with what you are quarreling about. It may be a memory of something else. But all the same it's a quarrel. One remark leads to another. Accusation follows accusation. Nastiness turns to meanness.

"Maybe you don't need me," I said—and this just after we had made love.

"Let's not talk anymore," she said. "I know what's coming."

She did. *She* had that sixth sense.

"Maybe," I said, "what you need is an Arab prince."

Now why did I say that? There must be another person inside all of us who says these things.

"Oh, so that's what this is all about. Well, sweetheart, maybe what you need is a million dollars. Fix you right up."

"No, I'm not the one who said *let's do it.*"

"But you're the one who thought it and don't tell me otherwise. You were willing. You still are. Listen to you go on about Philadelphia, and now this Friedrich. You think I don't know what that means? You want out, Josh. Say it, Josh—say you want that money!"

"Let's stop this, Joan, before we do permanent damage."

"I never started."

"Stop it, Joan!"

"You actually struck a man today. What does that tell me?"

"It tells you I've had enough. Okay?"

"You need another vacation."

"That's exactly what Jules said."

"Well he's right."

"Is he also right about me working for a Nazi? An Adolph yet?"

"That doesn't make him a Nazi. Adolph is a common name in Germany."

"You can say that again."

"Josh, you're just looking for an excuse."

"An excuse for what?"

"To quit your job."

"That's no secret."

"So quit!"

"Then what?"

"You know darn well what."

"Send you off for breeding?"

"I see no other way out. We've only been back a few days and it's already tearing us apart. Think what it'll be like in days to come."

"It'll get better."

"It'll get worse. I know you, Josh."

If only, I thought—if only I hadn't stopped in at the Versailles. If only I hadn't responded when he had called me over for *good luck*. If only we hadn't had dinner with him. If only I hadn't gone up to see him later on. But I had. The answer was yes to all of the above. The trap had been set and I had stepped right in. Hello, I had said, did you advertise for a sucker? Well here I am. But really, who had set the trap? Maybe it had been me. After all, I knew what I was doing. All along I knew what I was doing. *I* had set the trap.

No, I had not known what the price would be. So in that

sense I was blameless. But from the beginning I knew there'd be a profit in Ibrahim, a man so rich that the leftovers he scattered behind could plant a thousand fortunes. So I had played him as surely as he had played me.

True, he had seen us first, caught a whiff of that gorgeous wife of mine on the casino floor of the Galaxy and was smitten. Then—with the help of Sy Rodrigo—he set out on a campaign to win her, first by luring me to his blackjack table at the Versailles. How did he know I'd be there at the Versailles? I could have been at ten other casinos that day, or none at all. That was a mystery. No figuring that out.

But it was also true that I had seen him before he had ever seen me or Joan. Somewhere in my life, I knew there'd be a messiah. I had no idea what shape he'd come in. I certainly had not figured on an Arab. But I knew there'd be a savior to gather me up and deliver me to a land of plenty.

The next day I had lunch with Adolph. Just the two of us, plus Jules Corson. Jules would not trust me alone with Adolph—or with any client, really. The purpose was to get acquainted. Knowing that I was allergic to fish, Jules had made reservations at the Philadelphia Fish Company on Chestnut. I filled up on bread.

"Josh here is very excited about writing speeches for you," Jules said to Adolph.

Jules never lied. He also never told the truth.

"I am so happy," said Adolph.

"Josh is our best," said Jules. "He's written speeches for senators and governors."

"Ah!" said Adolph, nodding in polite admiration.

Jules was just making conversation. It was always difficult with a client. You had to be charming and entertaining and you could never relax. But you had to act relaxed. That was what made it so difficult.

"But I am not a senator or a governor," said Adolph. How about a führer? I thought.

"Oh," said Jules, "I was just giving you some background on your man."

"I already know his background. I am very impressed." Say thank you, I urged myself.

"Thank you," I said.

"There will be many speeches to write," said Adolph.

"Josh doesn't mind," said Jules. I don't? "He's looking forward to the challenge." I am?

"Josh," said Jules. "Did you know that you'll be traveling the country with Mr. Friedrich?"

"No, I didn't know."

I had thought I'd be writing a single fill-in-the-blanks speech, an "evergreen" as we called it in the business. But no, I'd be writing a separate speech for each plant visit.

I had done that once before with another CEO and it had been a two-week nightmare, sharing breakfast, lunch and dinner with the same man—a man who, by the force of being a client, owned rights to your every mood.

Most unbearable were the "plant tours" I had to submit to. Machines pounding, grinding, mashing. You were obliged to wear hard hats here, protective goggles there; and the foreman, over all that din, kept explaining things and you kept nodding in fascination, though you couldn't hear a word. "Oh really?" you said.

"We will be spending much time together," said Adolph.

"Josh is looking forward to that," said Jules.

"Maybe you will even teach me good English," said Adolph. "You will be my expert."

"Josh wasn't even born in this country."

I knew he meant well; but why, I wondered, why did Jules have to bring that up? This wasn't smart.

"Oh? Where were you born?"

"In France," I said.

"You must have been very young when you left."

"I was."

"Why did you leave?"

Jules said, "Josh left after the . . . when the . . . because of the . . ."

"The war," I said.

"Ah!" said Adolph.

"Josh was too young to remember anything," Jules said by way of dismissing World War II. "And besides, his whole family got away," he added by way of dismissing the Holocaust.

"Not quite," I said. "Most of my family, in fact, perished at the hands of the . . . the . . ."

"The enemy," said Jules.

"Ah!" said Adolph.

How do you talk to a German about the Germans? I had never had this before. As for Jules, he was experienced in making history disappear. Once, when we were pitching a Japanese account, he deleted his entire war record from his résumé.

I had always had trouble with that, as I was having trouble with this. To let the past be the past was fine with me, but to trade in your medals for the sake of business—well it made sense, it was *practical*, but it stunk.

So to make amends quickly, I now said, "The enemy, of course, being the Nazis."

Jules laughed—the laugh of a man who had just been kicked in the balls.

"But not all Germans were Nazis," he hastily explained.

"Ah!" said Adolph, who didn't seem to mind either way.

"Most of the German people did not know what was happening," Jules continued, now giddy from panic.

"That is so," said Adolph, still unruffled.

Jules's eyes sought mine to deliver a message—shut up or I'll kill you! Your job depends on this! No, not your job. Your life, you motherfucker!

"That is not so at all," I said. "Every German *knew*."

Now the odd thing was this: Adolph had done nothing to ignite this exchange, except for being Adolph. No, Jules was at fault and so was I. This was between the two of us. Adolph hardly figured.

Adolph could sense as much, so he had remained aloof. But that last remark of mine shot him down.

"All Germans were Nazis?" he said, screwing his eyeballs into mine.

Blink! I could hear Jules thinking. Blink, you son-of-a-bitch motherfucking cocksucker, or I'll kill you not once but twice.

So here was the question: were all Germans Nazis? Even a better question was this: do you tell the truth, at least what you believe to be the truth, or do you say what's good for business? Or do you hedge? You don't have to say *all* Germans were Nazis. You could say a *few* or *some* or *many* or *most*.

To say a few or some—either would be safe. Adolph would approve and Jules would rejoice. Yes, there were a few Nazis in Germany, maybe even some. Nobody would be so foolish as to insist that there weren't any Nazis in Germany. The evidence was too formidable.

A million-dollar account rested on my saying a few, some, many, most or all.

Adolph repeated the question: "Are you saying all Germans were Nazis?"

I was about to say "many," but my father stopped me. His image formed in my mind and he said: "For this I carried you across the Pyrenees? To cower before your tormentors? To *compromise*? Did Abraham our father compromise? Did Rabbi Akiva compromise? To compromise is to be true to two gods. There is only one. To compromise is to be *false*. Shame!"

My father came to me often, in a number of guises— the man of action gathering up his flock and shepherding them to safety between the fires of the Holocaust; the pious man, bent over his books; the frightened man, unable and unwilling to understand this new world; the defiant man, his fist raised to the heavens in protest.

What was he protesting? I was never sure. There was the obvious. He'd been routed from country to country, beginning in Poland, where the goons had taken his father to the village square, wrapped him in his prayer shawl, and set him ablaze as he cried, "Hear O Israel, the Lord is our God, the Lord is One." He'd been made to witness that, at a time when he was a yeshiva boy complete with sidelocks, which he shaved when he arrived in Paris.

In Paris he met my mother, the daughter of an aristocratic book publisher, bred three kids—and prospered. Big factory in the leather trade. Then the Nazis came. For a price—such deals were still made in the beginning of the Occupation—for a cut of his profits they would have let him keep his factory. He declined. For a price he could have left behind one or two of his children in the safety of the church, on the thinking that to split a family would assure that at least some would survive. That too he declined. We would all make the escape together. No, he'd never been one for compromise. It was all or nothing.

Even later in Montreal, and even much later in Philadelphia, he refused the handouts that were made available to refugees. Yes, refugees. Now he was a refugee again and perhaps that caused his great silences, silences that stretched out like the desert Sinai. Without provocation he would enter the kingdom of silence and remain there for weeks, sometimes months.

Was it something that he saw? Something that he heard? I used to wonder as a child. What did he know that I didn't know? There was a secret, a hidden outrage. Something spiritual, Biblical. Did he hear from Abraham,

Jacob? Did he see Isaac? Did he see Isaac on Mount Moriah?

Whatever he knew was not of this world.

He died with the secret; but the outrage, that he passed on to me.

"Yes," I said. "All Germans were Nazis."

CHAPTER 16

JOAN WAS being entirely too cheerful. Sometimes I wondered if there was depth to her. She seemed suffer-proof. Out there on the Main Line they pasted a smile on your face and sent you out to meet the world camera-ready.

She was the product of manners over feelings. She wept, she bled, but she mended so speedily that I doubted her capacity to know true emotion. Or maybe I envied her show of steadfastness against life's trials.

Where I came from people *anguished*. Ships and planes moved the remnants of a generation from continent to continent. Trains gathered up loved ones. The parent became childless. The child became an orphan. The wife became a widow. The husband became a widower. The patriot became homeless. Separations, farewells, reunions quickened the days. People knew great upheavals, great sorrows and even great jubilations.

But Joan—Joan was a child of peace. Sometimes I needed conflict. I sought the drama of my youth. Not

Joan. Joan sought harmony, which, idiot that I was, I often mistook for complacency—because Joan was deeper than I would ever be. She knew—and this was the only difference—she knew how to manage pain. She *made* herself cheerful. The worse things got, the more cheerful she became. This evening, before I even had a chance to bring her up-to-date on Adolph, she was more cheerful than I had ever seen her.

She had heard from Ibrahim.

"Oh?" I said. "Just like that?"

"Just like that."

Why, I wondered, was she being so triumphant? That should be bad news, not good news.

"You seem pleased," I said.

"Oh I'm very pleased. Shouldn't I be? Not every woman can say she's worth a million dollars."

"Surely he didn't mention money to you."

"Oh yes he did. It's quite clear that I'm the merchandise in this transaction."

Her smile widened to include a million dollar's worth of resentment.

"There is no transaction," I said.

"He's madly in love with me, you know."

"How flattered you must be."

"Oh, you can't imagine. One night with me would keep him for a lifetime. That's what he said."

"Are you about to start crying?"

"Me? I've never been so happy."

"I don't think you're happy."

"Of course I am. My husband has made a million-dollar business deal. Of course I'm happy. I'm thrilled."

"We never made a deal."

"He said you did. Very much so."

"That's a lie."

Ibrahim was a genius. He had planned that, too. To tell Joan that I had agreed. That could only divide us and surely send her to him, if not for the money, then for the defiance. From one faraway glance and a single follow-up dinner, how perfectly he knew her.

He saw the rebel in her that I never knew. Appearances did not fool him. She was not a contented woman . . . what woman was? What woman lived without forbidden yearnings and fantasies? Ibrahim knew Joan from knowing women. But Joan he mastered in particular. He saw right through her, beyond the layer of sunniness and directly into her naked heart.

When I told Joan about my lunch with Adolph—well, that was the clincher. There was no doubt now that I had insulted him with malice, on purpose, the purpose being to lose my job and force a desperate situation that could only be resolved in Atlantic City, in the bed of Ibrahim.

"You, you're the manipulator," she said, "not him."

Anyway, I had not lost my job. True, Adolph had been startled by my accusation that *all* Germans were Nazis, and Jules had hid back a fit, but it all ended without bloodshed—or worse, losing the account. Adolph's response was mild. He said he could appreciate how I felt. He said, further, that hatred against any people was unjust, but that he was willing to forgive me.

"*You* are willing to forgive *me?*" I was about to say, but Jules had had enough.

He gulped down some water and began to choke. He had performed this trick once before when another conversation with another client turned grim. This time I thought he was really going to die, so vehemently was he coughing, gagging and gasping, both hands at his throat. His eyeballs were about to pop out.

Everything in the restaurant came to a stop. The waitress rushed over with the manager, while I slapped Jules on the back, administering first aid to the best of my knowledge. I had once taken a company course in CPR. But now, when it came time, I forgot everything. Worse, I got mixed up between what you were absolutely supposed to do and what you were absolutely not to do.

Everybody shouted out advice. Stand him up. Sit him down. Bend him frontwards. Bend him backwards. Loosen his tie. Punch him in the spine. Punch him in the belly.

"Give him water," said the manager.

"That's what did this," I said.

"Water?"

Later, when just the two of us were back at the office, Jules denied that it had been an act.

"You're trying to kill me," he whispered.

When word got around that I had saved his life—for that was how I had spread the word—I was reprimanded by the entire staff, except Myer. No, Myer was jealous. Jules, according to Myer, would now be indebted to me forever, heaping on me raises, bonuses and promotions.

"You're his hero now," said Myer.

In a sense I was. Adolph, before goosestepping off to

his room at the Holiday Inn, had told Jules in private that he admired me. I was *such* an honest person. Business needs more men like me, he said.

"Now you and I both know that business needs *fewer* men like you," Jules said. "But you won the guy over. You never know with clients. But someday you'll kill me, Josh. I know you will. I'm on your list."

Actually the entire public relations profession was on my list. I got into the business while I was with the newspaper and was making a reliable dollar. I needed something unsteady. I'm that sort. A fast-talking but well-meaning politician persuaded me to write his campaign speeches. The catch was that I'd have to quit my newspaper job.

To offset that was the possibility that someday this politician might become president of the United States. He promised to bring me up with him and make me secretary of state. How could I turn down secretary of state?

So I accepted. First, of course, he'd have to win the congressional seat he was after. He lost, and not only was I minus secretary of state, I was minus a job.

So I decided to start my own business. The speechwriting business. I placed an ad in the classified section of the newspaper, advertising myself as a speechwriter for all occasions.

The people who needed speeches written, it turned out, were white supremacy advocates, loonies who wanted to declare Pennsylvania a separate nation and sex therapists who had everything but a diploma. The ad—it brought them out like a full moon.

My life as an independent speechwriter lasted exactly two weeks, and before I knew it I was working for Jules Corson in public relations, where nothing was sacred and everybody was scared. I'd never seen so many frightened people in all my life.

So many times I had thought of quitting. In fact, I once did. I saw Jules and I said:

"Jules, I resign."

He laughed in my face.

"Presidents," he said, "resign. You don't resign. You quit."

"Right. I quit."

"You can't quit. Get out of here."

So I'd have to get fired. I devised scheme after scheme. Anything to rouse me from this complacency and impel me to go out there and *do something*. So I arrived late for work, left early, took two-hour lunches, ignored memos, failed to show up for new business meetings, refused to join the Birthday Club, defamed my colleagues by declaring them useless to their faces, publicly ridiculed computers, made sexist remarks in the presence of feminists, and even fell asleep in the conference room while Jules went on and on about expense accounts.

My conduct with Adolph was my most brazen attempt, but it was nothing special.

So Joan was wrong about my motivations, although who was to say what lurked in the subconscious?

This much was true: I could not imagine myself touring the country with Adolph, a Nazi who was prepared to *forgive me*. Nor could I imagine enduring the routine of another day in Philadelphia, Slob City USA. For this I was born?

Surely the creator had something loftier in mind. What I had in mind was to excavate in Jerusalem, take part in the dig for the City of David. Find the radiance of my past. Maybe even find David or something about him that would lead me to his faith. I wanted to emerge from a cave utterly changed, divested of my earthly soul, aglow from spiritual transformation. That was my dream. Not *this*.

The twentieth century was not my idea anyway. There was no place for me here, where men deceived themselves into importance by devising Towers of Babel in the form of mighty computers and buildings that reached for the heavens.

And the view from heaven? What was the view of earth from up above? With all his doings, his comings and goings, could man be distinguished from the mole? For all his motion, where was he going?

If anything motivated me this was it—the need to escape futility. But how?

CHAPTER 17

IBRAHIM! Now here was more than a man. This was a force that controlled lives—could not revive the dead, make the lame walk or the blind see, but could make the poor rich. That power alone made him supernal.

We were being watched by him; of that I had no doubt. This was the same Ibrahim who had counted how many times I had let the phone ring in response to his dinner invitation. So of course he knew the turmoil now shattering our home. Miles away as he was, he even knew the dialogue.

But there really was not much more to say. There was no need to pronounce it or announce it—it would be done. By Joan, for her reasons. By me, for mine. There was no particular moment when we both arrived at the same thought and concluded it by word. That would have been too gruesome. Rather, we jointly surrendered to the inevitable and allowed ourselves to drift along.

But what was the protocol?

"Do I give you away like a father of the bride?"

No, said Joan. A limo would be here to pick her up.

"When?"

"Tonight."

"Tonight?"

"Better to just get it done, don't you think?"

She had already settled the details with Ibrahim. That was how inevitable it was. The limo would pick her up and deliver her to his suite at the Versailles, she'd spend the night with him and in the morning collect the cash. One million dollars!

Meanwhile—what does the husband do?

"Get drunk," said Joan as she packed her things.

How did it come to this? I wondered. From where did she win the indignation over me?

"If you're going to be angry with me then there's really no point to this."

"Please," she said. "Let's just survive this night. We'll be okay. We'll be okay."

I sat there on the bed, watching her, loving her, hating her, and searching for a precedent—trying to find a precedent for all this. But there was no precedent. *This* was the precedent.

"I think we should talk some more."

"All the talking's been done," she said.

"How do you feel?"

"Josh, Josh, Josh. You'd love a dramatic scene right about now. But you're not going to get it, so relax."

"Relax."

"Yes relax. I am not being raped, or even sold, really.

♠ 184 ♠

I'm simply doing what has to be done. You know it and I know it—and he knows it. This has to be done. That's final. Even up in heaven they know it, Josh. Yes, we're making a bad angel."

She had read in Adin Steinsaltz that every good deed created a corresponding angel. So did every bad deed. A bad angel came to life for every sin and these later testified and so you were judged, your good angels against your bad angels, and though Joan believed none of this mysticism she thought it such beautiful poetry that for that reason alone it had a right to be true.

She laughed. "Can you imagine the angel we're about to create? Talk about grotesque!"

This was sick and frightening, this thought, farfetched as it might be, that we were actually giving birth to something, a being, a being that would live forever in our name.

"Think of all the good deeds we'll have to do to get even," I said.

"Oh no. This is irreversible."

"So why are we doing this, Joan?"

"Oh, because life is funny, Josh. Life is funny."

"You do sound bitter."

"Uh-uh. Determined. I won't be swayed from this because this is it, our chance."

"You always said wait for my talent."

"Yes I know I said that but I've begun to agree with you that life isn't always so fair. It isn't right, Josh, what they've done to you, keeping you down, unrecognized and underpaid, and I know what it does to you going to

♠   185   ♠

work like that each day. You die every morning when you go to the office and I've begun to die with you—okay? So that's why we're doing this, Josh, because we don't want to die, not while we're still alive."

"This thing we're doing, Joan, it's bound to have repercussions. It could still be a death."

"Well . . . we'll find out."

Questions I could not ask: Was it all for money? Was there no lust? No adventure? No "once"?

She said, "Let's just do this night and get it out, *out* of our lives!"

Right she was. Do this night. Survive this night. Get it out, *out* of our lives.

"What did you mean by irreversible?"

"Only that it will always be something we did and we'll never totally forget it, but we're strong, Josh, we're both very very strong and we'll overcome it and be as happy as we once were."

"I don't know."

"Well I do. Nothing will change between us."

"I don't know."

"Time for me to say something corny, Josh. There's nothing stronger than love."

"I'm not so sure, Joan."

"Well if there is we've all got troubles. Josh, I'll always be yours. But if you ever decide to leave me, just tell me where you're going and I'll come get you. Yes I will."

"Me leave you?"

"It happens," she said.

"You will come back," I said.

"Not only will I come back, I'll love you more than ever. Will *you* still love *me*? That's the question."

"I'll love you more than ever."

"I'm not so sure," she said.

"Nothing you can do can make me stop loving you."

"So, there we are. It's perfect. Something ventured, something gained. We'll be as we always were. That's all I want. That's all I want, Josh. For us to be as we always were. That was so good."

Yes it was, and the past few days had been torture between us. This thing, yes, it had to be done.

"Why are you packing your negligee?" I asked.

"It's a nightgown," she said. "Not a negligee."

"But it's see-through."

"What are you doing, Josh?"

"I don't want you putting your heart into this."

"I'm not. Just my body. I told you."

Some more questions I could not ask: How many times this night would they mate? Would she climax? Scream from ecstasy? That was mine! That was supposed to be *mine*, the whimpering and the screaming. Would she get down on her knees and perform fellatio? That was also supposed to be mine.

Plain old sexual intercourse—for some reason that did not bother me so much. Not now. After all, it was so universal. It did not belong to me or to Joan and we could not patent it for ourselves. But the whimpering and the screaming—that was *territory*. The act of lovemaking I had already given up for this night. But the sounds—if she gave him the sounds, that would be clear betrayal.

♠ 187 ♠

* * *

The long black limo pulled into our driveway at eight. We said no goodbyes. The doorbell rang and out she marched, briefcase in hand. I watched her slide into the car, the chauffeur standing at attention until she was seated and then getting in on the driver's side. I tried for a parting glance but the windows of the limo were too heavily tinted. I could not see her but she could see me—which was about right for this entire business.

I galloped down the stairs and drove off in our Malibu and caught up with them on Roosevelt Boulevard and Harbison, followed them over the Tacony Palmyra Bridge to the North-South Freeway and onto the Atlantic City Expressway. I had no idea why I was doing this.

The limo was doing seventy with imperial ease and my car was clattering and complaining. The urgency I felt was that of a soldier rushing to battle, and I had to agree that it was easier being a hero in war than in peace.

CHAPTER
18

As I KEPT the limo in sight I thought, Do I want to watch? Is this what I want? No, of course not. I did not want to see her in her night with Ibrahim. But I did want to be near her. Proximity, for some reason, became important, as though by being nearby I was not relinquishing her fully.

But damn how I loved her!

The limo drove up to the Pacific Avenue entrance of the Versailles, and one of Ibrahim's men opened the door, helping her out and taking her valise. There was nothing hesitant about her movements. She was going at this boldly, as was her style once she had her mind made up.

There was still time for me to rush out and rescue her. But there was nothing to rescue.

I thought of all the times she used to say to me, "Do something!" Plenty of times I did much but not enough to please her. *Do something*, she said when we were on Seventeenth and Market in Philadelphia and a bum was shivering on the pavement and I—along with everybody else—had stepped around them so many times it never occurred to me to do something. But *do something*, she said, so I gave him a dollar and she added ten.

Do something, she said on Callowhill when two big kids had jumped a small kid in a parking lot. And I went over and did something.

Those were the days when she thought all the world's problems could be solved by *doing something*, when she resisted the big-city acquiescence of leaving it alone, the surrender that said if that's how it is, that's how it has to be. Not for Joan.

But now, do what? This was according to plan, the plan moving along act by act. Roles had been assigned and this now was mine, to watch her disappear.

I drove to the Galaxy, had them park my car and asked for a room. The registration lady was named Margaret Mailer. I said, "That's a famous name." She said for sure. She'd been here from day one.

She made me fill out the forms and when it came to how I was going to pay I handed her my Master Card. She punched it up in the computer and then made a phone call and gave me the bad news. I was past limit.

She tried to be nice, Margaret Mailer. She asked if I had other credit cards. Sure I did. I had plenty of credit cards. But the rest were also past limit.

This was like the time Joan and I went furniture shopping at Gimbel's a month after we were married. We spent five hours choosing this and that, and then that and this—the salesman skipping his break and even his dinner for the fat commission he saw coming.

In the end, after we had bought virtually the entire floor, he made the phone call and came back to report that our credit was no good. It ruined his day, poor man.

But there was more. He ordered us up to the credit department. A very angry lady was already prepared for us. She asked to see my credit card. I handed it over. She lifted up a pair of scissors and cut it to pieces in an act of public disgrace. An auto-da-fé, this was.

Someday, I later told Joan, we would get even. We would have so much money that they'd be sorry—and wasn't that the whole purpose behind this night, this night with Ibrahim? To get even with Gimbel's, Straw-bridge's, Wanamaker's, the phone company, the gas company, the electric company, Visa and now Master Card? That's why she was up there, to end the humiliation of being middle-class poor. Once and forever.

After tomorrow there would be no more of this. We'd go cash all the way. That was no fantasy. Not anymore. That was how it would be, starting tomorrow.

Meanwhile, though, there was today. The big *now*.

I used Sy Rodrigo to get a room. After all, he certainly had used me to gain much more—Ibrahim's business. For that he had given away my name and identified Joan, which was not really much of a crime. What it was, as Ibrahim had said, was an *understanding*. That was how the world was run from the top, by understandings.

So I mentioned Sy Rodrigo to Margaret Mailer. She made another phone call and this time I was approved. In fact, the room would be comped, but only for one night. That was fine.

"By the way," I said, "you're not related to the real Mailer, are you?"

"I *am* the real Mailer," she said.

By golly she was.

I had no luggage so I did not need a bellboy to escort me to my room, and that saved me a few dollars. I had sixty-two dollars on me. I could have had more but I had left the house in a hurry!

Now in the room I fell back on the bed. Sleep would be the best thing. If only I could sleep this through. Wake up and it would be over. Then it would begin, the mending and the forgetting. The money would not take care of that.

By this time, I thought, the preliminaries were being done. Drinks, music, getting acquainted. Ibrahim was not the sort to rush in. Or was he? As soon as she walked in—maybe it started as soon as she walked in.

So by now it was *done*—at least the first one, and there was still a long night ahead. There would be no sleeping for Ibrahim. This was his night. There were a million dollars to be used up in Joan. No, there would be no sleeping for Joan, either.

Or for me.

Maybe, I thought, it would be best to go down to the casino floor and use up some of my money. I would not care about winning, not when I had a million dollars coming to me. I only needed the action. Something to keep me busy. The slots would do, and wouldn't it be something if I won the million-dollar jackpot? Then I'd know there was a God, but not a nice one.

No, the best thing to do was sleep to kill these hours

between Joan and Ibrahim, so I flicked on the TV, picture without the sound, got in under the covers and—sleep? Are you kidding? I thought. She certainly is not *sleeping*.

I remembered back then when the Sabbath-school teacher said, "and he slept with her," and me—age ten at the time—wondering, so? What's wrong with a man and woman sleeping together; unless, of course, you mean . . . you mean they weren't actually *sleeping*.

Walking with our hockey sticks to join the others in the lane on Esplanade, Maxie, much older and wiser at twelve, said, "You're crazy. You actually think when it says they're sleeping, they're sleeping? They're not sleeping, Josh. They're fucking. Where you been all your life?"

"So why doesn't it just say that?"

"You're an impossible kid, Josh. You actually want the Bible to say fucking?"

"No, but the rabbi . . ."

"You actually want the *rabbi* to say fucking?"

"No, I mean . . . it's not clear."

"It's clear, Josh. It's clear. To the whole world it's plenty clear. You? I don't know."

"But sometimes it does say he went in unto her."

"Where did he go in, Josh? In her ear?"

"I'm not that dumb."

"Yes you are. If you ever grow up you'll learn."

"Learn what?"

"That everybody fucks."

Of course this was nonsense. Only bad people did this, like the guys outside the poolroom and the guys in those shiny suits and Wildroot hair twirling their keychains

♠   193   ♠

outside Herm's Candy News and Soda Shop on Fairmount Street. They were hoods, so it figured.

But who were the girls they did this with? I couldn't
think of one girl who would do such a thing. Even Maria,
the girl behind the counter at Herm's who wore those
tight white sweaters and always whispered to the guys,
she was only *teasing*. That's all girls do. They just tease.
They never actually do this. I mean fucking is not for girls.

Later, however, I had to admit that people actually did
this—but only glamorous people. Like movie stars. Marilyn Monroe probably did this and maybe Errol Flynn,
though not Jeff Chandler. He was Jewish. Therefore not
Lauren Bacall either. She was only teasing Humphrey
Bogart.

Maxie insisted ugly people did it too. You put a bag
over her head. But suppose he's also ugly? There were
plenty of those guys around. Put a bag over both their
heads?

As for beautiful Joan, I was now thinking, she was only
teasing. I even pictured her, up in his suite there now,
suddenly confronted, suddenly *aware*, throwing her
hands up to her face, gasping as in those silent movies,
saying, "Oh my! You didn't really think . . . You don't
really expect me . . ." Then: "I was only *teasing*."

But this Ibrahim, he would not know from teasing. This
was not your basic Uncle Harry from the Bronx getting his
jollies from a pat to the tush. This was *Ibrahim*! Sultan or
something from Mahareen or someplace. Your genuine
full-blooded billionaire. Teasing was not this man's style
and, come to think of it—it wasn't Joan's style either.

Once she decided on something . . . once she decided on doing her "once" . . . it was as good as done. Oh yes.

Like the time before we were married and I was feeling so guilty about everything and called her to break the date, to break the whole thing off, even saying I didn't love her and going on and on; and after all this, this whole speech, as if she hadn't heard a word, she said, "I expect you here in twenty minutes. Goodbye."

But now . . . imagine this! Ibrahim, *going in unto her.*

I had no rightful claim to these thoughts since I had willfully abdicated her for this night, had given her away, and was much, *much* to blame. In fact, it was entirely my fault. Imagining what they were doing—this was an intrusion. Yes, *cheating.* To be feeling sorry for myself was a solace I did not deserve.

But still, going in unto her . . .

Escape this room, I thought, or you'll start tripping downhill like that night at the Marriott in Dayton, Ohio, when you realized there's nobody in the whole world. Every man, you decided, is an island.

Damn her and her "once," and damn me and my craving to be rich. What a collision!

Would there be scars, I wondered . . . were we, yes . . . were we creating an angel?

"Watching?" she had said way back when we were just getting familiar and talking in general. "Nobody's watching. You're a mystic."

"If nobody's watching, why do people do good things?"

"Because people are good."

"Oh no. Because somebody's watching. At least that's

what people think. Good Christians cross themselves in private, don't they? *They* think somebody's watching. Good Jews whisper when they pray. *They* think somebody's listening and watching. So somebody must be watching and taking notes and writing down license plate numbers."

"Ha!"

Only she could say Ha quite like that . . . a rich girl's Ha, like a rich girl's shoulders and a rich girl's legs and a rich girl's hair and a rich girl's . . .

In unto her. Oh yes definitely. In unto her.

Like this? she is saying.

Like this?

Then in the struggle reversing the Ha to Ah . . . ah . . . ah . . . ah . . . ah . . . ah . . . ah . . . ah . . .

"I mean," said Maxie, "you think they're actually sleeping? Jesus Christ, Josh. They're *fucking.*"

CHAPTER 19

SO TO GET OUT of the room and kill time—yes, almost literally every fucking minute—I took the elevator down, and in the lobby were four hundred million people from some kind of convention, all gabbing and laughing and wearing the same clothes, corpie suits even here in Atlantic City; and on each lapel and breast was pasted a sticker that said Visitor, and for some reason I found that hilarious.

I said to one guy, "Is this a philosophical statement?"

"A what? We're with the convention."

"I mean we're all visitors on this planet. Is this what you're saying?"

"You must be crazy."

Maybe I was. I was feeling crazy. The casino itself was half empty, blackjack dealers standing alone and bored before their outstretched cards waiting to be shuffled. There were even two-dollar tables.

But I could not zero in because of this crazy feeling. So what if I won? So what if I lost?

So what? So what? So what?

For crying out loud, we're just fucking visitors.

In making my rounds, in and among the blackjack, the roulette, the craps, the baccarat, the Big Wheel, around and around, back and forth, speeding past faces and faces and faces, all so tough and joyless, I was like a swimmer who had gone in too far, too deep and once too often, and was now madly stroking for life.

Make sense of something, I warned myself. Quickly. Insanity is next.

Think of something nice. Like what? Your wife? That hurt. Your father, your mother, your children? That also hurt. Think of the money. That hurt the most. So think of Jerusalem. Okay. That was nice.

Next year in Jerusalem—with Joan.

Are you all right? I asked myself. Now are you all right? You're not going to die now, are you?

Are you all right?

Is he all right?

Don't touch him, somebody said.

I don't think he's all right.

I was not flat on my back. I was in a sitting position. So I had not fainted. Only collapsed. My legs—they were so weak. Could not support me. Just like that they gave—and I sat down. I had not fallen, just sort of came to a stop.

I had been walking too fast, around and around. I had gotten dizzy. That was what this was, a dizzy spell. Another dizzy spell. Big whoop, as Joan would have said. If she were here. But she was not here, of course. No, Joan was not here.

Joan was busy at the moment.

"Are you all right?" voices said.

"Is he all right?"

Men and women in uniform were ringed around me. The same thing had happened to me in Jerusalem on day six of the Six Day War. I pitched hand grenades as we charged to the Wall. Then something hit me and I was carried into an ambulance. A bearded man asked me my name. "Joshua," I said. "Aha," he said. "Do you know the story of Joshua?" Yes I did. "Then you know about the twelve stones." Yes, God had ordered Joshua to place twelve stones in Jordan as a memorial for the deliverance to the promised land. "So what we must do," said the bearded man, "is place twelve stones by the Wall."

I had taken a bullet right through the kneecap and spent six weeks in the hospital. When I got out I could not find the bearded man. I asked about him. I described him. Was he a doctor? A chaplain? Nobody knew who he was. So I did it myself. I gathered twelve stones from Mount Zion and placed them by the Western Wall. They had to be gone by now, but in my mind they were still there.

Now the man who seemed to be the leader of the group said, "Can you get up?"

He stretched out a hand. I reached for it and pulled myself up, but when he let go I was down on my ass again. My legs seemed to have forgotten what they were intended to do.

"That does it," the leader said, and in my blurred condition I had no idea what he meant.

Were they going to line me up and kill me?

Is that what they do when you can't stand up to gamble anymore?

To collapse in public had always been my big fear—next to being confined. The shame of it, more than anything. But there was no shame here. No, everything continued. I had collapsed beside a craps table where the action was loud and furious and on it went—"Come on seven . . . come on seven . . . bring it in, sweet baby!"

People from the casino's Emergency Care Unit now arrived and they were alarmed. Very concerned about me. Loosened my tie, took my pulse as they moved me along in a wheelchair. What was I doing in a wheelchair? I did not remember them seating me in. This is awful, I thought. I'd seen the crippled come here as if to Lourdes to be healed, but never the other way around, like me, walking in and being wheeled out. Sort of the opposite of being healed.

Still, there was dignity in all this. This was like a presidential procession, sentries at attention along my route, information being passed about my condition by walkie-talkie—and even an elevator held just for me. All because I could not stand upright anymore.

Why could I not stand anymore? Because I had heard the voice of God.

This was what He said: "Joshua?"

Already I knew that was bad.

When He loves you He calls your name twice: "Moses . . . Moses," He had said.

But I just got one: "Joshua?"

"Here I am," I said.

"I am cutting you off from your people, Joshua."

That was when my legs gave.

Now I was never one of those who claimed to hear from God, and I still wasn't. That was my father talking to me—my father, since he died, had become God. That was how I imagined God, as my father. Quick to anger, slow to forgive. That was how I saw my father. That was how I saw God. My father's face, harsh but loving, loving but harsh, became God's face.

But I could separate them. I knew when my father spoke to me as my earthly father, and when He spoke to me as my heavenly father. This time He had descended on me through a whirlwind in a blazing chariot.

I am cutting you off from your people.

They had me down on a bed now, in a room full of lights, a nurse taking my temperature. She asked me if I was cold. I said yes. She spread a blanket over me. I said the wool itched. She did not hear me. They seemed to choose when and when not to hear me.

She asked me what was wrong.

The thing was, I wanted to tell her! Everything. I wanted to tell her about Joan, what Joan was doing right now—and what I was doing. I wanted to tell her what I had done.

What have I done? I thought. How could I have done this? Where *do* we go from here? This is the beginning of something and it is the end.

I wanted to tell her that I was being cut off from my people. I was no longer under the protection of the covenant.

"What's wrong?" she said.

"Nothing," I said.

"Anything hurt?"

"No."

"You have no fever. But your heart is racing like a child's."

Was I on drugs? she asked.

"I take Valium occasionally. Fiorinol for migraines."

"Do you have a migraine now?"

"No. Nothing."

"Why can't you walk?"

"I think I can walk now."

"No, you stay here and rest."

"How long?"

"We'll see. I'd like the doctor to take a look at you."

I shut my eyes against the lights. Think good thoughts, I told myself. Bad thoughts are what kill you. But— what was Joan doing now? I saw her naked, down on her knees . . .

I threw the blanket off me.

The nurse rushed over. "I thought you were cold."

"I'm hot."

Hot and cold was what I was.

"The doctor will be right over."

"Can I have something to put me to sleep? All I want is sleep."

"The doctor can give you something."

I waited. So where was this doctor? Everything, I thought—everything is taking *so long*. Things are happening in the world and here I am, wasting, my flesh devouring my soul. A malady of the spirit this was.

The doctor was a skeptical old man. He had the blithe

attitude of a professional who had already seen everything, seen so much that nothing could surprise him. He had people categorized by type. His name was Moore, Dr. Horace Moore.

As he examined me he kept up a chatter.

"I hear you want a sleeping pill. Just one, I hope. I have people come in here wanting more, if you know what I mean."

"Just one," I said.

"I get them after they've dropped their entire life's savings. Gambling is not for the fainthearted."

"I didn't lose," I said. "I won."

"Hmm. I get those, too. They can't handle that, either. What did you win? A million dollars?"

How did he know? Of course he didn't know. A million dollars was that magic number.

The American dream. The American jackpot.

"You're a sick man," he said after he checked my eyes.

"How sick?"

"I don't know. But you have the symptoms of shell shock. Were you in a war or something?"

"Many years ago, yes."

"No, I mean today, yesterday. Now there is nothing physically wrong with you, but . . ."

But, he said, he saw something, something he did not like.

"You need rest," he said.

"Can I have a sleeping pill?"

"You really want that sleeping pill, don't you? That's also a symptom."

"You just said I need rest."

"Rest doesn't mean sleep. Rest means . . . you know what rest means. You're fighting something. What are you fighting?"

"I'm not sure I understand."

"I'm sure you do understand."

"You want a confession of some sort?"

"No, I'm only a doctor. My stethoscope can only reach your heart. Your heart of hearts, that's something you know. You and God. Anyway, I'll give you that sleeping pill. But that won't be the answer."

"Thank you," I said, "that's all I want."

"Yes, the sleeping pill." He paused to look me over, human to human. That was something he obviously did not do too often. "I'm worried about you," he said. "You know, I was in a war myself. World War Two. I saw what people do to other people. That's sad. Now I'm here and I see what people do to themselves. Guess what? That's even sadder."

A confession, that was what this man wanted from me.

"You're one of those," he said.

"One of those?"

"You know what I mean. Here . . . here's your pill. Just remember, it's not the answer."

CHAPTER
20

WHEN I GOT BACK to my room I took the pill with water and waited for it to work. Sleep was so important to me now. More important than life. I gazed out the window and even from this distance, in the dark of night, I could see a bearded man on the beach walking his dog.

I dropped myself on the bed and finally drifted off to sleep. I slept for about an hour. When I awoke my eyes were burning. My throat felt hot. It was two in the morning and not a good time to be up.

I had had a dream. In this dream Joan and Ibrahim were at the foot of the bed laughing, mocking me. I knew it was a dream but I also knew that they had been here. I was sure of it.

In his final days, living alone in Philadelphia, my father used to say that people visited him in the night. He wrestled these people. I did not believe him, of course, but the furniture all over the house *was* overturned.

My father even showed me the bruises of his nocturnal

combats. I chose not to believe him because to believe him would have opened up the lower world, and I chose not to believe in a lower world.

Now I glanced around and I sensed the special emptiness of a room that had just been vacated. People had been here, been here and left. In one form or another, Joan had been here. I could smell the fragrance of her perfumes and could see the shadow of her smile. Ibrahim had been here.

Chairs were out of place. The phone was off the hook. Blankets were scattered on the floor. There had been a struggle. Between me and Ibrahim or between me and myself?

Possibly I had rioted in my sleep. But I was tucked in under the covers. I had fallen asleep on top of the covers—or so I remembered. I was in my shorts. I had no recollection of undressing. The second pillow—I *knew* I had not touched that—was indented from what appeared to be two heads.

I was sure of it—they had been here, been here and made love in my bed as I slumbered. What a perfect touch! The bonus. For the contribution of a million dollars Ibrahim was not about to deny himself this added satisfaction.

But Joan—how could she have taken part? Did she despise me that much? Maybe so. This, this thing that I had done was so low that God had never even thought of it for His ten or even His 613 commandments. He had made provisions against murder, robbery and adultery—but this?—never.

Yes, right here on this bed they had made love. Right here Joan had been vibrating under the cover of another man, the sexual pleasure made doubly intense by the fact of my sleeping presence.

As for Ibrahim—why? I had never done him harm. This was supposed to be a straight business deal. Why the mean vengeance? Maybe this was an Arab-Jewish thing after all.

No, I thought, this was no grudge. Kicks, that's what this was. A billionaire—how does a *billionaire* get kicks? Since everything is his to begin with, he must be desperate for new pleasures. He must improvise new sensations.

Nothing could be more perfect than to bring Joan here, in my bed.

But how did he know I was here? Well stupid, I said to myself, think! You had them call Sy Rodrigo to get you the room. There's your connection. To further ingratiate himself, wouldn't Sy pass the word to Ibrahim that I was here? Of course he would. Sy would have no misgivings. He was part of the deal. In fact, he was the first conspirator.

But Joan—what a reversal of form! What a transformation of character for her to consent to something so utterly debased. Consent? Maybe it had been her idea in the first place. Who knows where passion ends once it begins? Kicks, she was also one for kicks. *Once*—she believed in trying anything *once*.

There was only one thing for me to do. Reject the thought. Otherwise I was cut off not only from my people but also from Joan, and Joan was all I had. Joan was my sanity in all this chaos and I had to trust her, trust her goodness, trust her love in the face of this sordid adventure.

There was nothing else to do. To delve further into this conjecture, to believe that Joan was capable of such scorn, would leave me with nothing but madness. This time for real. No false alarm, as before. Before had been a warning. Maybe a beginning. Joan was good. Joan was beautiful. Joan, whom I had betrayed, Joan, who had betrayed me—Joan would have to be my savior. Joan would have to restore my soul. She alone could raise me back up—both of us together. Up, up, back to the land of the living. For this was *sheol*. This was the valley of the shadow of death.

So I had to dismiss the evidence as fantasy, imaginings provoked by guilt.

But *somebody* had been in this room besides me. I knew that. The eyes were still here. I lunged out of bed. Got dressed. Went to the bathroom. Did not even wash my hands. Did not check myself in the mirror for fear another face would stare back at me.

I dashed for the door, thinking it might be bolted to everlasting. Thinking I might be trapped here for life to spend my days in confrontation against myself.

Then I ran for the elevator. I had to get down to the casino to prove to myself that it was real, that it had not been another set-up to confound me. The corridor was empty. The elevator was empty. Was the entire world a set-up?

But finally—now I knew what I had to do. I had to rush over to Joan and tear her from Ibrahim. That was what I had to do. Now. This was enough. I had to cheat him out of one more screw and deprive myself of my million dollars—for the deal would be broken if I cut him from his full night. That would make it almost right, almost fair, almost bearable, almost forgivable.

I was on the eleventh floor. I pressed the "casino" button. The doors closed and down I went. Then the elevator stopped between floors. I waited. I pushed the "casino" button again. Then I pressed the "emergency" button. Then I picked up the emergency phone and dialed the emergency operator but there was no response. Now I pressed all the buttons and I was on the move again, but upwards.

The elevator stopped at twenty-two, or between twenty-one and twenty-two, and so this was it, I was finally stuck in an elevator and it was like that business in *Nineteen Eighty-Four* where they find out your worst fear and do it to you.

For Orwell's guy it was rats, and for me it was this, and I was sure I'd never get out and that Ibrahim was behind all this, and Sy, too, and paranoid was I? Of course.

Worse than stuck, the elevator began to bounce, zooming up and down, changing speeds as if someone, some human, were at the controls and as if the elevator itself were human or had a brain.

For some reason I was not as frightened as I should have been, though I was flustered when the two doors parted an inch or two and clamped shut just as I tried to power them apart, and here I was, here I was, like that time in the Pyrenees, bound by straps inside the tiny rucksack my father carried me in on his back. I was even gagged, some

♠ 209 ♠

kind of cotton stuffed in my mouth to keep me from crying and alerting the Germans, who were all over the place with their dogs.

Even when I retched nobody knew, they were so busy fighting the wild, almost sixty of them, terrified men and women and their young, branches and twigs snapping in their faces They had to keep a fast pace behind the guides, who only now and then let them stop to rest. And then it happened, just as I knew it would. My father put me down and when it was time to move on again in the dark, he picked up the two valises he'd been carrying. But in the haste and confusion and panic he forgot the rucksack, he forgot *me*, and here I was and couldn't even scream. I watched them disappear.

Now it was the same and the elevator stopped moving. I tried the buttons again for each floor—and nothing. Over and over and no response again and again. I even tried shouting, first Ibrahim's name and then Sy's. Then, after I gave up the shouting and sat down and a great deal of time had elapsed, I tried something else, prayer, which I had not done in years.

I said, "Hear O Israel, the Lord is our God, the Lord is One."

Hours passed, and I was three-quarters asleep and only half lucid—dozing on the floor of the elevator that was becoming a coffin—and in this stupor I conjured up King David, my very own King David. He came to me in those white robes, his face beautiful and kind and so radiant and so strong, and I said: "You're not here to reprove me, are you? You're my guy."

"You're my guy, too. Thou art that man just as I was that man."

"We're talking you and Bathsheba?"

"No we're talking you and Joan—and this Ibrahim. What have you done?—and don't tell me the woman made you do it. Adam already tried that with the One who is, was and always will be."

"Oh no. I have sinned a great sin."

"I know how it is, Joshua. You did it for money. I did it for love."

"You mean it's okay?"

"He's ticked off at you, Josh. Why an Arab? Why an Amalekite? You know He doesn't like them!"

"I got tired of waiting."

"He was going to make you rich, legally."

"He was?"

"Oh sure. You were inscribed in the Book of Wealth."

"So what was taking so long?"

"You know what my son Solomon said. He said 'In the morning sow your seed and in the evening do not be idle, for you cannot know which will succeed, this or that.' For you, Josh, it was coming in the evening. If only you had waited and trusted your talent as Joan kept telling you. In good time, Josh, it would have come to you in good time. If only you had waited."

"We don't have all the time in the world—not like He does."

"You lost faith, Josh. That's the biggest sin of all. And an Amalekite?"

"So why make them so rich?"

"You're judging *Him*?"

"I'm only asking why give them all the oil and everything?"

"That's His business."

"Why does He make them hate us so much?"

"They don't all hate us."

"Oh no? Does He watch TV news? Does He read Anthony Lewis?"

"He created Anthony Lewis."

"Talk to Him about that."

"We're here to talk about you. Pick a punishment."

"How about no chocolate for a month?"

"You've read my Psalms?"

"Who hasn't?"

"Funny? Would you call them funny?"

"No."

"Well this isn't funny, either. You know the Amalekites stole two of my wives. With Joan that makes it three. This Joan of yours—how could you sell her off like that? That's never been done before. You almost deserve congratulations. This is not only a great sin, it's an historic sin. The next time Moses goes up he'll come down with eleven, strictly on account of you!"

"There you go reproving me, David. It's not like you."

"I'm sorry. It's just that He liked you so much. He was nuts about Joan, even though she is a shiksa."

"He did? He liked me?"

"He loved you, Josh. He loved your folks, too."

"So He gave them Hitler?"

"His schemes are not our schemes, you know that, Josh."

"But now He hates me."

"He's thinking it over, and in any case there's going to be punishment."

"What?"

"I can't say."

"You're still my favorite guy, David."

"You're okay too, Josh. I forgive you."

"So bless me before you leave."

"I can't do that, Josh."

"You can't leave before you bless me."

"Yes I can and it was only Jacob who could wrestle an angel."

"All right. But just say this—Joshua Joshua."

"Can't do that, either. That's too much."

"Come on, David. Just once say it twice."

"Promise me this—to love the good and hate evil."

"I promise."

"All right, Joshua Joshua."

Now I was awake and it was morning.

CHAPTER
21

THE DOORS PARTED. A hand raised me from the void and pulled me out. I was on the casino floor. A wrinkled old man in a "security" uniform said, "How long you been in there?"

"I don't know," I said. "What time is it?"

"Ten."

"Day or night?"

He looked at me.

"It's ten in the morning, fella. What's going on?"

"You tell me. Don't you people check your elevators?"

"This is the bad one."

"Very bad."

He said he'd have to make out a report. He tried to lead me to some office but I refused to follow.

"Where you going?" he said.

"I don't know."

But I went out for air. The sun hung over the ocean like

a blazing yellow balloon. I still felt that terrible heat, a heat that kept me moving, straight for the Versailles.

Up on the Boardwalk, as I marched toward Ibrahim, I felt like a bum, not at all presentable, and when I caught a glimpse of myself from a shop window I decided to clean up.

But instead of using a hotel's facilities I headed down the beach to the water—the hotel would have been sensible and that was exactly what I did not want to be now. I kind of liked how I looked and felt, irrational and wild, and so I just cleaned up a bit down by the water.

When I got to the Versailles the casino guards gave me the once-over but let me in, and there he was, Ibrahim, at the same table, the same table where it had all begun. He still had that fierce majesty about him, and I was awed as before, except that now this was mixed with high indignation, the sort of power a man feels when he's been defeated and can be defeated no more. There's not much more they can do to him and so he can only win.

The table was roped off, but this early in the morning there was not much of a crowd to watch him. There was no crowd at all, in fact. There was only me.

I watched him play. He was doing everything wrong. He knew I was there, of course, but he pretended otherwise. He kept busting against the dealer and in no time was down a stack of millions.

Then his luck changed. Two blackjacks in a row and then the dealer began to bust. Ibrahim won the next eleven hands. I had never seen such a run.

What? What was it about me that brought this man such

luck? What was luck anyway? Was it designed from the heavens, or was it the one power that heaven did not control? Luck was perhaps the single force outside heaven's province. There was no calling it down by virtuous deeds or a clean life—it rested on the undeserving as capriciously as on the deserving.

Whatever it was, I had it—for Ibrahim.

Now he turned to me. "Again it's you," he said.

I stepped over the rope and sat down next to him.

The pit boss walked over to me and asked if I wanted to play. The minimum was ten thousand dollars. But now I understood. The million dollars had been placed in a casino account under our name.

This was the perfect way to do it, of course. There was no other way to do it. No cash, no check to openly violate Joan's honor and my dignity.

A class act, Ibrahim. Really, he was impossible to dislike. You could hate everything about the man, but you could not hate the man.

"No," I said to the pit boss. "I'll just watch."

"As you wish, sir."

Sir. They do not call you sir at the three-dollar tables. Well well well, I thought. So I'm a millionaire.

The pit boss came up to me again and said there was a suite ready for me in the hotel. Comped, of course. Free room, free meals, for as long as I wanted.

Now a free drink was brought to me by a lovely hostess. I did not have to ask, did not have to utter a sound. I was now part of the world that spoke in nods—and understandings.

In this world virtually everything was free of charge. When you are rich you do not have to pay. When you are poor you do. That's strange. But it's also part of the understanding.

After winning and then losing a few more hands, Ibrahim invited me to his suite, as I had expected and as he had expected. He knew I'd be back as I knew I'd be back.

This was not yet finished. Everything had been done, but something remained unresolved. Joan—and I did not ask—was surely back or on her way back to Philadelphia by now. If not, if she was still in his bed, we were then working on our second million.

My impulse should have been to drive straight home. Instead I was driven to Ibrahim. Ibrahim was first on my agenda. I had his money and he had had my wife and there were things to talk about. Could he feel pain? Maybe that was what I had to know. Because I was certain Joan had left him loving her. She knew no other way to leave a man.

The bodyguards were up there patrolling his corridors, and in some of his rooms business was being conducted. Men in desert garb were clustered around telephones speaking in urgent Arabic. I had not noticed that before, and I also noticed for the first time that there were no women. There must be women here, I thought, but they must know their place, wherever that place may be.

These were a different people, I had to remind myself. Their ways were not our ways. Their women were not our women. Their women were in bondage. They were kept in veils and kept separate not because they were weak but because they had such awful powers, the powers of temptation, the powers to corrupt.

That was important to remember. To Ibrahim, Joan was not a person. She was much more and much less. As much as he felt desire for her, equally as much he felt scorn for her.

She was *sin*.

Now in his room we were face to face.

He said, "No scenes of reproach, I trust. That would be most unseemly."

"No, I've been paid."

"So have I."

"Now that is unseemly," I said.

"I beg your pardon. Yes it was. But this—this meeting is so unnecessary."

He got up from his chair and poured himself a Pepsi. He did not offer me one. No, even hospitality was now so unnecessary. He did nothing to hide his boredom. He was not very attractive right now in the glare of the sun that shone in through the balcony window.

He was restless and irritable and the reason for it was plain. He had been up all night. His eyes were red and puffed up, his jowls floating. Flat nose, thick lips—this was not the earlier Ibrahim. He was a man who required prep time to work his looks and his charm. I had caught him unawares.

"It's a big mistake, your coming here," he said. "How many chances you think a man gets?"

"In an ordinary lifetime? One chance at everything."

"But no more. Consider yourself lucky, Mr. Kane. You're ahead. You're ahead, Mr. Kane. That's the thing about a dumb gambler. He doesn't know when he's ahead. Doesn't know when to quit. I hate gamblers like that. They weary me. They make me sick. I'm surprised at you, Mr. Kane. I was so impressed with you at the blackjack table. You knew just when to quit. The man matched you blackjack for blackjack and you knew it was time. I was impressed, Mr. Kane. But now? I am not so impressed now, Mr. Kane. Be a smart gambler. Get up from the table and get lost."

"It isn't time," I said.

"You keep trying me. Don't you know? Never look back."

"I know the rules."

"You're breaking the rules. You have no class."

"I have a million dollars. I don't need class."

"So take the money and disappear."

"This is not attractive," I said.

"No, it is not attractive. I like you, Mr. Kane. You look deep inside the human heart. This makes you touching. But it also makes you pathetic. Any man who looks deep inside people is asking for trouble. He'll find what you've found. It is not attractive. It is ugly. Take it from an expert. You know I'm an expert, Mr. Kane. You know this too well. I can play the game because I don't get hurt."

"Something tells me you do, Mr. Hassan."

"Oh in the beginning, yes. I'll let you in on a secret."

"I like secrets, Mr. Hassan."

"Good. The secret is this—I started playing the games

only after I found that not a single person could resist the power of my wealth. You think I enjoyed this, this discovery? You think I went chasing after them? They came to me, from the lowest to the highest, humbling, groveling, disgracing themselves. There was nothing they would not do. I could make any person do anything I wanted. *Anything*. Some lesson, huh? I thought, there must be one person, one individual somewhere, with real *dignity*. So that's the game, and now I enjoy it, because there is no such person. There is no such dignity. Oh false, bogus dignity, this we *all* have. Do you know what real dignity is, Mr. Kane?"

"It's what makes us but a little lower than the angels."

"Aha, King David, right?"

"Right."

"The Psalms. But *are* we but a little lower than the angels? Take it from me, this is one time your King David was wrong. The sweet singer of Israel he was, yes, but this is too sweet."

"It's bad money," I said, "that makes people such puppets. It's cheap power."

"I am not getting through to you, am I, Mr. Kane? It's not the money. It's the *people*. Isn't it sad? Haven't you learned anything in this life of yours? Well, learn this— Put your faith in money. Put your faith in God. But never put your faith in a man, and certainly never a woman."

I agreed with him as I agreed with the lunatics who harangued pedestrians from downtown street corners. Listen carefully. Everything they say is true. But they are still crazy.

"Isn't it really thrills?" I said. "Isn't that what you're really after?"

"From a deep person such as you, Joshua Kane, this is a surprising statement. I'm disappointed."

"It was a question."

"You want to know what motivates a man like me, don't you?"

"It is a mystery."

"So I'm telling you. It's a quest for dignity, this pursuit of mine. You've done your reading. 'One man in a thousand I have found, but one woman among them I have not found.'"

"I Koheles," I said.

"Of course. So I Ibrahim continue Solomon's search. Though I have not even found this one man in a thousand."

"But the woman," I said. "You found her in Joan."

"Oh yes. But the search goes on as life goes on."

I said, "It must be difficult, being so wealthy."

"You're saying this facetiously, and yet it's true. It's like being a god . . ."

"But how you flatter yourself."

". . . in the sense that all people stand naked before you."

"Oh, people are flawed and frail, Mr. Hassan. Who can quarrel? But is it really necessary to lure them into corruption? Isn't it really for the *fun* of it, for the *game* as you yourself admit, that you entice them out of their integrity?"

"I lure nobody, my friend. They lure me. Men—industrialists!—have fallen on their knees, begging me to have a *picture* taken with them, a handshake to show on the stock exchange. Worth gold! Women? The wives of religious leaders, even wives of prime ministers . . . they wait outside my door. You use the word corruption. Tell me, is any man or woman beyond corruption?"

"Mr. Hassan, I said I agree. We are all vulnerable creatures. But isn't it awful to *use* this, like using the testimony of a biased witness? I mean, isn't it cruel to plunder the human heart?"

"I would be unable to *use* this if people had dignity."

"But you yourself admit that only by a hair do we maintain our higher nature over the lower. It is a fragile balance. So why tamper? Why tip the scales? Why not leave it alone?"

A pause, then a smile. "Maybe you're right," he said. "Maybe it is for fun."

The real treachery here, I thought, was that he had such cause. I'd have liked him better without the justification. With justification everything was legal. This seemed to be the age for justifying—even Hitler and Manson, poor things.

So he found something out, this Ibrahim. Good for him. Found himself a truth: people are rotten and corruptible. So, stop the presses? No big secret.

He was silent for a while. Maybe, I thought, he has another secret.

"The movie," he said, "is that what you're worried about?"

The movie? What movie? No, I had not been worried

about that because I had never thought of that. A movie of Joan and Ibrahim? Forget the sordidness—it would make Joan his forever. A movie of this night to delight him in the days to come—no, that I had not imagined.

This would not be fair. The deal had been for one night. Now, with a movie, it would be for perpetuity. For all time on film he would be making love to her. That would mean that I could never put this night behind me. Neither could Joan. This night would go on forever.

Now it flared up again, the terrible heat I thought I had cooled.

There had to be a solution to this man, I now thought There had to be an answer.

"You made a movie?" I said.

"She didn't know."

"You made a movie?"

For the first time I had him on the defensive. Not quite, but his self-assurance was not as complete as usual. Due to the fact, possibly, that I was without fear and he could sense a recklessness in me. For the first time, *I* was dangerous.

She didn't know. Some comfort.

"Only for half an hour or so," he said.

"You have such contempt for me, for Joan, for yourself?"

"There is nothing wrong in preserving a moment—the most beautiful moment of my life, if you must know. No, not contempt. Precisely the opposite is true. I cherish Joan and I must keep her, and I can keep her by no other means."

"So you made a movie."

"Would you care to see it?" he asked.

This offer, as far as I could tell, was not made in a spirit of derision. No, he wanted me to share this film with him out of kindness. The film was his prize, the most valuable prize he owned. He had found a way of preserving Joan, of owning Joan.

So he saw nothing inelegant in all this. He had achieved something lasting with her, even more lasting, more binding than the vows of marriage. A film was always there, always faithful, always true. In his film he could have Joan over and over again as even I could not have her. So we were partners, as he saw it, and he wanted to share his bounty, partner to partner—and it was almost pathetic.

Not quite, because there had to be an edge of contemptuousness in this scheme. This meeting was his confrontation more than it was mine. This was his final satisfaction. I had no vengeance to return. Nothing that I could think of at the moment. But I would have to come up with something. Oh yes, I would.

From beginning to end—if this was the end—he had me ensnared. He seemed unbeatable. He seemed incapable of error. A chess player he was all right, who saw ten moves ahead to my one.

How, I wondered—how do I beat this man? How do I defeat this undefeatable man? I could not go on with Joan or continue my life until I beat this man. There must be an opening, I thought. Somewhere in this calculation of his there must be a miscalculation.

"I did not come here to see a movie," I said.

"Aren't you curious?"

"About watching my wife make love to another man?"

"I don't see it quite that way. I see us as two men joined by something extraordinary, if you agree that Joan is extraordinary, as of course you do. We both belong to her and she belongs to both of us."

"You are wrong, Mr. Hassan. Joan belongs to *me*."

"You forfeited her, Mr. Kane."

"For a single night."

"Oh no. Forever, my friend. Forever."

The same was true for Joan, I thought. She had no movie, but the memory would be there, could be there, forever. Memory was stronger than a movie. Memory could also be true and faithful, and it could also embellish and make a moment more powerful than anything in reality or anything on film. The film in Joan's mind, that was where I had forfeited her.

But Ibrahim's film was tangible. He was not enough of a romantic to rely on memory. He needed something actual to bring her to mind and revive his sensations. He needed the film to love her and have her love him. The film was worth more than a million dollars. Yes, the film was worth all his billions.

"On the other hand," I said, "yes, I would like to see the movie."

"I'll get everything ready," he said.

He rushed out and I heard voices, his in particular, loud and tremulous. This cool gambler, this impervious manipulator, was now as excited as a schoolboy. I was serene. I knew something that he did not know. I saw a move he did not see.

The limits had already been been reached, even surpassed. The unimaginable had already come to pass. The unspeakable had become speakable. There was nothing but to save what was left to save. Joan—I could still save her. Somehow, I could still rescue her from Ibrahim. I had been given a second chance.

There *was* an answer to Ibrahim. Joan was the answer. His foil was now my foil. His trap was now my trap. His weakness was now my strength. Mighty Ibrahim could be toppled by a woman, my woman, as I had been cut down by money, his money.

All I needed now was luck. For once, I thought, let my good luck be for me. I had given him enough. My turn. For once, I thought, let the winner be the loser and the loser be the winner.

I was not seeking revenge, only balance. Life had so tilted me that up was down and down was up. I was spinning in a world where right had become wrong and wrong had become right. Balance was all I was after. Perhaps, after all, the name for that *was* revenge.

Ibrahim returned with a servant who brought in a tray of soft drinks and nuts and left. No popcorn? I thought. Another servant brought in and set up the VCR machine and left. Ibrahim held the cassette in his left hand, the cassette worth his entire fortune.

Now I became as alert as a detective. I knew there were guards outside. So making a run was out of the question. The windows in here were sealed. But—but there was a balcony. The handle to the door of the balcony needed nothing more than a twist. The ocean was not that far off; it could be reached by a good throw, the kind of throw I had used in a previous conflict between Arab and Jew, when I had pitched hand grenades against the Jordanian Army as Israel fought to regain Jerusalem.

Correct, this was not an Arab-Jewish thing. This was man against man. I finally knew that—knew that he was no god. I had thought he was. That had been my mistake. I had made him a god by virtue of his money. But I no longer feared his money.

There was only one big question, and I could not ask it now. It would give me away.

Now he drew the curtains for proper dimness, inserted the cassette into the slot and it was showtime. I shut my eyes but this was a talkie and the sounds were the worst of it.

So I opened my eyes and beheld Joan—as I had tried all this night not to imagine her—kissing him from head to toe, stopping in between, her head bobbing as she sucked his hard, blood-filled penis. He was groaning and shouting out her name. She was nude and on her knees.

Now she gazed up at him, panting and smiling. He tried to lift her up but she wanted more. He cupped and squeezed her breasts and she reinserted his penis into her mouth and suckled.

Finally she let him lift her up. He grabbed her by the ass, stuck a hand in her ass, and placed her on top of him on the bed—and she slammed herself into him. Now she shouted—"Oh!" She began working herself in and out of him. The sounds, yes, the sounds were the worst of it—the gasps of ecstasy from her.

The view was from the rear. All I could see was her motoring ass, wide as the screen, wide as my entire world. Then he raised her and turned her around and as she pumped from a sitting position his left hand palmed her left breast and the fingers of his right hand were jammed inside her cunt along with his upright penis.

Now her face came into sharp focus. Her face now filled the screen expressing something animal. The secret he had seen in her, that secret was out. The passion he had suspected, the surrender, here it all was in a single female explosion.

She was glancing down to watch his penis move in and out of her, to watch herself being fucked.

This, I thought, was what they dreamed of on the Main Line, in their pink bedrooms.

Now she shut her eyes and grimaced, as though he had reached a new depth inside her, reached her heart. Her breathing grew hoarse. Now she helped him. She stuck one of her own fingers in her cunt and her cunt was as full and as busy as any cunt could ever be.

He lifted her off him and drew himself under her and licked her cunt. But she would not let go of his penis. She stroked it with her hand. He even licked her ass. His tongue moved from ass to cunt. Then it was time to come and he sat her into his penis again and again her face was in sharp focus. Her eyes were lined up with mine. I could sense contact, as though my presence were before her. Look at me, she seemed to be saying. Look at me.

But that was a presumption based on conceit. She was coming not for me, but for him. Her lover. Her screams were not for me, but for her lover. This was all for Ibrahim. None for me. Not even in spirit, not even in mind.

The climax was violent. She yelled out his name, as if for mercy. She yelled out his name.

I glanced over at Ibrahim. This final moment was his perfection.

"Enough," I said.

He clicked off the machine. He was quaking. His eyes had turned menacingly black, void of the spark that separated the human from the beast. He was silent. He seemed to be containing the savage in him. But he could kill. Now I knew that he could kill.

As for me, no, it had not been pleasant. But I was beyond the hurt. I had girded myself for this. I knew there were times in life when there were no choices, and that this was such a time. I had had no choice but to sit through this outrage. I had had no choice but to witness the finale. The sin had been mine and this was the punishment. The ultimate punishment. *This*—this was *midda-keneged-midda*, measure for measure.

But I had had enough of sin, enough of punishment.

"Do you have copies of the film?" I asked.

"You want one?"

"I might."

He thought this over. It seemed logical to him that I should want a copy. After all, we were partners.

"I'll have to make some copies," he said. "This is my only one."

That was it! The big answer.

Damn, I had wanted to hear that!

I edged toward the VCR machine. He did not seem to notice me. He was depleted, his mind distant. The contents of the film still had him gripped. He was lost in a state of sublime amazement.

"I'm happy that you understand," he said.

"I do. I understand."

"You are a witness."

That he needed. A witness. A witness to validate this and make the film true.

"This is holy," he said.

Holy, I thought. If this is holy what then is depraved?

"Yes, this is holy," I said.

I kept inching closer to the machine.

"Tell me," he said, "was she ever like this with you?"

Yes she was, I thought. Yes she was.

"No," I said. "Never."

Humor him, I thought.

"Are you sure?"

He wanted proof. Maybe a film. That was important to him, to know that he had reached her as I never had, as no man ever had.

"Yes, I'm sure."

"That's good," he said. "I asked her to stay with me, you know."

"Oh?"

I had been afraid of that, of course, afraid she would stay with him. I had counted that as the worst outcome, never figuring on a film. I had not been prepared for an eventuality just as bad, or even worse. In effect, she *was* staying with him.

"She refused," Ibrahim said. "But I have the film. You see—I have the film."

"Yes, the film."

"The film is everything. But only you can understand. You do understand?"

"Yes, I understand."

"The film is a memorial. No, come to think of it—I cannot make copies. There must be only one."

"Fitting," I said, "for a memorial."

"Yes, there must only be one."

Now I was within arm's reach of the cassette, the memorial, the one and only. I swung my arm out just to test the distance. When the moment was correct, I thought, I should be able to snatch it in one motion. A single movement would be all I'd get. If I fumbled he'd be on top of me.

"Joan knows nothing of this."

"So you told me."

"Do you think me cruel?"

We were beyond cruel, I thought. We were talking perversion.

"No," I said. "Everything makes sense."

"Yes, everything is as it must be. Everything is right."

He turned to the window, his back to me.

I thought of making a lunge for it now, but he was between me and the balcony. He would have time to stop me. There would be a struggle. Maybe I would win. Maybe I would lose. An even shot. I did not like the odds, especially with the guards out there ready to pounce.

No, I would have to proceed swiftly and suddenly when all was perfect.

But I had to move while he was still in this melancholy.

"Only a woman," he said, "could do this to a man."

Now the other side, the hatefulness.

"Do what?"

Keep him talking, I thought. Keep him talking.

"Hold such power!"

He sat down and lit a cigarette; not a cigar, a cigarette. For once he was not posturing. His inner self was his outer self. The mystique was gone. The prince was earthly.

"Look what she's done to you," he said.

He wants my *pain*, I thought. He wants to see my pain. He requires my assent and my pain for his satisfaction. To be a true witness I had to rejoice for him, despair for myself.

Be smart, I thought, and give it to him. Give him anything. He is yours anyway. All yours.

"Yes," I said, "look what she's done to me."

Never mind what I had done to her.

"Man's blessing and man's curse, that's what they are," he said.

Like money, I thought.

"But you've been blessed," I said.

"Yes, there is only one Joan."

Yes, I thought, and there is only one film. I drew it from the machine—gracefully and perfectly I reached out and made it mine. I clutched it against my belly, then slipped it in my side pocket.

Ibrahim snapped to life. "What!"

"Now it's time," I said.

He knew the stakes. This was for everything. As I had

gambled once too often, so had he. In the end every gambler was a loser and he, Ibrahim Hassan, had finally extended his luck too far, spread it too thin. This one last wager had been for all or nothing and he had come up busted. The movie, that wretched, putrid movie, had delivered him to me.

He stretched out his arms to block my path to the balcony. He was now completely back to his senses, and now was the moment to yell out to his people—but pride muted him. He was a black belt, after all.

I held my arms loose to the sides and did not take up the forward outlet stance. As he swayed and shadowboxed around me, he put on the meanest face he had but his breathing came fast and loud. I had reverted to battlefield demeanor, which dictates that they cannot kill you since you are already dead.

I wondered which way he'd be coming so I faked left-right and we began to circle and stalk. He tried a shuffle straight kick to the groin and I simply rocked back, unscathed. It had been a halfhearted effort on his part, merely to test my reflexes.

I knew I was rusty and that I'd have to trust the credits that had accumulated in my brain. To Imi and the other professionals, Krav Maga was religion. Trust it, always. Can a simple lifting and rotating of the arm really block *any* roundhouse? Always, if you do it right and study it and study it as the others study Torah. Can the system really make you sublime? Why yes, so long as you carry it humbly within yourself, as any wisdom. "So a man may walk in peace," was Imi's proverb. We had had a mild disagreement when he proclaimed that Krav Maga should be open to all. "Share the secret with our enemies?" I said. He thought by sharing it our enemies would become our friends. A charming naiveté, so typically Israeli.

Ibrahim continued to stalk and withdraw without landing or taking a punch or a kick, staying safe, playing the menace, setting up combinations that were supposed to terrify me.

I had been in these things maybe five thousand times, mostly in drills on my way up from white to yellow to orange to green to blue and then to brown belt. In these spars the other guy was not your opponent. He was your partner. Over and over again you practiced the same moves, different moves, hundreds of them, until they became instinctive. A few times in my life, of course, it was for real, and these were different. You never knew what the other man had.

In a flash Ibrahim stepped in, flared left-right whipping blows—karate chops—wheeled and connected with a spinning roundhouse kick that grazed my chin. Terrific speed, and I paid for being lax. I was staggered but unhurt.

Now I brought my arms together, crossed, for an outside defense, to lure him wide. He bought it, stepped in, faked a left hook and swung a right-arm roundhouse. I rolled the punch over my curling left arm, ducked swiftly at the same time, torqued and planted a fist to the ribs. He flew back, prancing.

I had had him doubled over for an instant and was in position to finish him off with a hammerblow between shoulder blades, and it vexed me that I had not gone in for the score. It occurred to me that the opponent I was facing was me. I lacked killer instinct. Even now. Damn this thing compassion. So *Jewish*. The Israelis had solved it, to a degree, by constantly showing and reminding the boys what the goyim had done to their ancestors throughout the ages, and it helped, but after turning the other cheek for two thousand years it was something new to be learned, and what is learned is never the same as what comes naturally. But it was also true that once they got going they were ferocious. Menachem Begin was right when he said, "They want a holy war? We'll give them a holy war."

I had the same thing in mind now when Ibrahim came leaping with a scissor kick. I remembered my back roll and when I straightened up I was against a wall. I lifted a knee and got him flush in the groin. He was hurt but still quick, falling back, recovering and taking up his attack stance.

I was still reluctant to attack. I preferred to get him on his mistakes. From a safe distance now, he resumed shadowboxing and it was comical. I had to laugh.

"Come," he said. "Come."

Never laugh, I thought, at an able-bodied man.

"Come," he said. "Come. Teach me."

Must have a big move in mind, I figured.

I sped in, finally, with a crossover side kick, which he blocked. I spun and wheeled a back kick, connecting heel to chin after faking low. He switched to boxing combinations, two straight lefts and a hook followed by two straight rights and a hook, six times. I was counting. None landed but he was impressive.

Good form, I thought. Good style. The seventh time I exploded in, both arms high, left blocking his right hook, right smashing into his nose. This was good. Exactly by the book. He also had a book. As I was moving in, my momentum carried me too far and he caught the back of my head with a horizontal elbow blow. Now I knew this was a fight. Never mind judo and karate. He knew Krav Maga.

He noticed the blood from his nose and charged wildly. I stepped easily to the side, bullfighter style. He charged again, throwing a flurry of whipping blows. I blocked them all by use of the 360-degree defense—all but one. This landed in my ribs and doubled me over. I was in this position when he delivered an uppercut that sent me reeling across the room.

I backpedaled around the room to recover and kept backpedaling close to the walls to keep him centered and in view, except that I could not find him. I could not see him, the poor sucker. He was gone. I wondered what did it. Something from before?

I felt fine. The dizziness was natural and so was the nausea and the fogginess. I felt fine, and then I felt kicks and blows to my head, groin and chest and this last one, to the chest, took my breath away and I collapsed.

I came around, possibly from shock, from this awareness that a killing was about to take place. He continued to kick me as I lay there and it was obvious that compassion was not one of this man's flaws. He was an Amalekite. *Do not forget.*

I struggled upwards and managed a lunge at his midsection, which merely served him my head. He grabbed me in a headlock and this, I could tell, was his finish, as those massive arms continued to squeeze and squeeze until I felt my eyes jamming my brains. Hell, defense against headlock had never been my specialty and was, in fact, what had kept me from the black belt, and I tried to sort it all out in my mind, what was left of it.

That special move against headlock, what the hell was that sonofabitch thing? Avri had taught it to you, I thought, a hundred times. Even warned you, "You must know this." This wasn't even brown or black belt material. It was white belt, what they taught you in the very beginning. That was perhaps the trouble. It had been so long ago. I never took it seriously because it was one of those street-fighting grabs. I didn't think of the headlock as a death-hold. I placed my mind on rewind and got back to Pardes Chana and imagined it was Avri holding me like this, not Ibrahim.

"Step out with the other man's momentum," Avri said. "Step wide."

Now it came. The whole thing. All I needed was the beginning. I stepped out wide, making his movement mine. As I inclined downward I slapped him in the groin with my right palm. He loosened and as he did I straightened and pulled his head back with my left, coming around back by his hair.

He was open. I came across with a right-hand blow to the neck, wheeled back taking his right arm with me, clasped the hand in my "69"-shaped palms and twisted the wrist until he went down, down, down, down to his knees, terrible affliction rising from the heat of his face.

The good old Cavalier.

"Am I doing it right?" I said.

Pathetic, having this god down on his knees, all mine. Two voices shouted inside my head, the one saying *compassion*, the other saying *kill him. Kill the son of a bitch.* A kick to the throat and finis.

Remember, I thought, who this is. *You know who this is.* He is from now and he is from before, he is from here and he is from everywhere. Remember *their* compassion.

"Am I doing it right?" I said, tuning it up another notch.

Let flash before you all that your young eyes have seen and all that your ancient soul has witnessed.

Up another notch.

He tapped his leg. Over and over again. The pain had him gasping, his mouth fishing for air.

Then it was too late. We both heard the snap at the same time. His wrist went limp.

A horrible cry rose up from the depths of his throat.

But I was out of time. I heard them at the door. I rushed for the balcony. The handle refused to give. I stepped back and booted it ajar. They were in the room now. Down there was the ocean, the waves coming up big. I wound up and as I did I yelled out, "Kadima, kadima!" Then I heaved the cassette and hollered, "Alley." Plunk. Made the first wave. They had me surrounded and were about to do something but Ibrahim stopped them.

"Not him. Not him. The film. The film."

They cleared out and dashed for the elevators.

I also decided it was time to go.

CHAPTER
22

THEN THERE WAS Sy Rodrigo. I owed him. I went up to him by way of the same elevator that had trapped me. The *bad* elevator. But it was not so bad now. Sy's secretary said he was on the phone. Before, that would have made no difference, but now I was commanded to remain in the outer office. So I waited, and I waited.

"He's very busy this morning," said the woman.

"I only need a minute."

She disappeared into his office. When she came out she said, "He'll see you now."

Sy was not his usual self. So formal all of a sudden.

"Rough morning," he said. "But you know how it is."

"Yeah, I had a rough morning myself, Sy. You know how it is."

"I heard you were in our dispensary. Listen, I did not mind comping you to a room again. But I am curious. I mean, you're welcome here and all that, but why *are* you here? Is Joan with you?"

"Joan is back in Philadelphia, Sy. She also had a rough morning."

"Rough all around, huh?"

"Mind if I sit down?"

"I can only give you a minute, Josh. I've got a speech to get out."

"Then I'll stand. Do you mind if I stand?"

"No need to take that tone with me, Josh. What's up?"

"Who's the speech for?"

"Oh Stavros, our president. He's giving a talk to a group of visiting travel agents. The usual."

"You're writing the speech?"

"I wish you were. You're the expert."

"I'm very good at writing speeches."

"I just said you were. What's going on?"

"Yes, I would like to write that speech for you, Sy."

"Thanks, but it's my problem. You don't know what to say, anyway."

"Oh, but I do. Like the truth, maybe. Wouldn't that be a change?"

"You know a truth, Josh? Remember it's me you're talking to. Your friend Sy. I know all the truths. You know how? By knowing all the lies."

"Can you still tell the difference?"

"I don't need this from you, Josh. Please leave."

"*Do* you know the difference?"

"Maybe I don't. Maybe there is no difference anymore."

"I'm here to tell you that there is."

"Good for you. Now please go. Let's keep this friendship."

"I could lose my privileges, couldn't I?"

"Yes, yes you could. Why are you doing this?"

"No more freebies, huh?"

"Come on, Josh. What happened?"

"Something happened, Sy."

"Obviously."

"Something very bad happened. People were hurt."

"An accident?"

"On purpose."

"Well don't come here laying blame on me. I didn't do anything."

"I didn't say you did and I'm not here to lay blame."

"So what do you want?"

"I'm a high-roller now, Sy."

"Oh? Congratulations. Hit the jackpot?"

"Maybe you even know how."

"No, I don't know how."

"Isn't that what I mean? You don't know a truth from a lie."

"We traffic in lies, Josh. That's my business."

"Speaking of business, here's what I intend to do. I intend to deposit a million dollars in your bank, right here in the Galaxy. I may gamble none of it, or I may gamble it all. In either case, I'd be the highest roller you ever had, potentially speaking."

"Yes, you would be."

"I mean, high-rollers, that's what it's all about."

"Correct. That's what it's all about."

"Who do I see about depositing this money?"

"Me."

"You don't seem surprised by my new wealth."

"You say you've got it, Josh. That's good enough for me. Anyway, nothing surprises me."

"Suppose I went directly to Mr. Stavros."

"It's your prerogative."

"What would he do to net a *quality* player like me?"

"Anything."

"So we're finally talking price, Sy. You and me. A million dollars. Would that be his price?"

"Stavros?"

"Yes."

"A million dollars? Yes. I'd say that's his price."

"He'll do anything for that money."

"Anything."

"Would he betray a friend?"

"For a million dollars, yes. Anybody would."

"Are you his friend?"

"We're close."

"Well that's the price, Sy. That's the exchange."

"*What's* the exchange?"

"You, Sy. You for a million dollars."

"Me? You want me fired?"

"Absolutely."

Terror emptied his face of all expression. Saliva dripped from his mouth. Now it was plain to him and it was plain to me, too, how frail he was—him and all the rest of us.

I had him now, the man who had sold me and my wife to buy Ibrahim. Now Sy was mine, mine to buy and sell. That had been King David's prayer. *Make me wiser than my enemies.* Well, I was no wiser. I just got lucky.

♠   244   ♠

Ibrahim had said it for me. Luck is everything.

This was supposed to be the end of the line for Sy, this job. No more shilling for wrestlers and roller derby queens. Public relations director for an Atlantic City casino hotel—that was a satisfying conclusion to a checkered career. He was home.

No more chasing after newspaper columnists. They now came to *him*. He even had comping rights, so *everybody* came to him. He had power. Now that power was turning on him.

He said, "I concede that you have the power to ruin me, and I'm sure you have your reasons. But will that make you happy, Josh? Will it make you happy to ruin me?"

A moment ago, yes, it would have made me happy. I had been so sure. Now, however, I was convinced that no revenge would be the greater revenge. Spare him, I thought, and let him know that money is *not* first. Something else is first. Something else.

CHAPTER
23

WHEN I GOT HOME she was in her favorite place, the shower.

"Is that you?"

"Yes," I said. "Is that you?"

"Cute."

"Is it coming off?" I said.

"I didn't hear that remark."

She came out wet, shiny, naked and happy, and after she got dressed she said, "Where were you?"

"I had business."

"Hmm," she said.

"What does that mean?"

"Whatever you want it to mean."

"When you say hmm it means something."

She said, "Of course it means something, silly. But I won't tell you what it means."

"It's very sexy when you say hmm."

"Hmm."

"What happened?" I said.

"To me?"

"Yes you."

"Ha!"

"What happened?" I said.

"You're something."

"I want to know what happened."

"Of course you do," she said.

"So?"

"Nothing. Nothing happened."

"Nothing happened."

"I told you. Nothing happened."

"I know different."

"Oh you know everything," she said.

"Just some things."

"I suppose he told you."

"He didn't have to."

"You believe what he tells you? He's a liar. They're all liars. What were you doing there anyway? Look at you! You had a fight, didn't you? Why are men such boys? Did you beat him up? Did you beat him up *good*?"

"Broke his wrist."

"Ha!"

"I did."

"That make you the champ?"

"You're being a million-dollar bitch."

"Aha."

"Say hmm."

"Go wash up. I'm making dinner."

"Just like that, you're making dinner."

"Take a shower."

"We're supposed to sit here and eat dinner."

"Yes," she said, "like ordinary people."

"Like nothing happened."

"Nothing happened."

"I saw the movie."

"What movie?" she said.

"He made a movie."

"Baloney!"

"He made a movie. I saw everything."

"You did not. You saw nothing."

"Everything."

"Good," she said. "I fulfilled my end of the deal. All right? All right?"

"All right," I said.

"I did what I was *paid* to do. All right?"

"Fine."

"Where's the movie? I want to see that movie."

"I destroyed it," I said.

"How?"

"I just did."

"There was no movie. You're bluffing. You're a bad bluffer. There was no movie."

"All right. There was no movie."

"But you hate me," she said.

"I don't know."

"Oh you don't know. Wonderful."

"It's too soon," I said.

"I guess so. It's too soon for me too."

"This will take time."

"You bet," she said. "But don't take too long."

"Is that a threat? Are we talking divorce?"

She said, "I thought we promised never to use that word. Remember? We said there were certain words you must never use because when you use them they have a way of becoming fact."

"So is it fact?" I said.

"I didn't say divorce."

"All right. I said divorce."

"What about all that money we suddenly have—split down the middle?"

"If it comes to that, sure. The money . . ."

"I don't want to hear about the money."

I said, "You brought up the money."

"You brought up divorce."

"What's the difference?" I said. "We're rich."

"Aren't we happy to be rich?" she said.

"Very. I cannot tell you how happy I am."

"You sound very happy," she said.

"That's because I am very happy."

"So am I. I'm so happy."

Later I said, "Joan, I don't know where we go from here."

"How about a suicide pact?"

"Now there's a word you should never use."

She said, "You don't know where we go from here!"

"Where do we go?"

"Where everybody else goes," she said.

"Where's that?"

"I don't know. You just go on. People just go on."

"Where? I want to know where?"

"You're crazy," she said.

"Go where?"

"There's nowhere to go, Josh. You just go on."

"I see."

"You see?" she said.

"No I don't see."

"We pretend nothing happened."

"Pretend?"

She said, "Survivors pretend. That's how they survive."

"Pretend what?"

"Pretend nothing happened. Like Holocaust survivors."

"This was no Holocaust, Joan. Don't give it that honor."

"All right, it was a small Holocaust. But it was ours."

I said, "You can't live a lie."

"Why not?"

"I don't know. It's what they say."

"Sometimes a lie is good," she said. "Sometimes a lie is better than the truth, if it's a lie of compassion. Compassion is better than truth. Right now, Josh, we don't need truth between us. We could use compassion. Now am I still your shiksa or what?"

Jerk, I said to myself, tell her she is.

"Too soon," I said.

"You're a schmuck," she said.

CHAPTER
24

IN THE DAYS that followed she repeatedly asked me about the movie and I assured her I had only been bluffing, there was no movie, but it had her troubled. I was sorry to have brought it up and justified it on my indignation, the urge to get even. I reminded myself, when the fire of my moods subsided, that all the real getting even had been done, and besides, the vengeance I pursued had no face, no shape, no name.

But my moods were terrible and I hated life. I tried music and it failed. Even Beethoven turned German on me. I tried reading and found this from David's son: "I, Koheles, was king over Israel in Jerusalem. I applied my mind to seek and probe by wisdom all that happens beneath the sky—It is a sorry task that God has given the sons of man with which to be concerned. I have seen all the deeds done beneath the sun, and behold all is futile and a vexation of the spirit. A twisted thing cannot be made straight and what is not there cannot be counted.

"I said to myself: Here I have acquired great wisdom, more than any of my predecessors over Jerusalem, and my mind has had much experience with wisdom and knowledge. I applied my mind to know wisdom and to know madness and folly. I perceived that this, too, is a vexation of the spirit. For with much wisdom comes much grief, and he who increases knowledge increases pain."

Joan accused me of self-pity and I agreed, saying it was good. It was the realization of the ultimate truth—you against the world. But, I said, I pitied everyone.

"Does that include me?" she said.

"Of course."

"Does that mean you forgive me?"

"In time."

"Well I forgive you, Josh. I have no hard feelings."

That was the difference between us. I pitied everyone. She forgave everyone.

A whisper told me if I played the tough guy much longer she'd turn tough herself—and when they turn tough it's over.

She wanted to go back to work. Instead she stayed home. She redecorated the house and cooked meals that took her three hours to prepare. We spoke but not much. She kept eyeing me.

On *Sunday with Frank* he sang about this thing that died, a little thing called love, and she rushed to turn off the radio. Then she started cleaning the house again and I remembered that TV station I once worked for, always last in the ratings, and how they kept changing the news-room set.

I was surprised. I mean she had never been Mrs. Home-maker and now all this, cooking, baking, cleaning, shopping. She—the lady so willing to try anything once—now said there were boundaries in life, a circle beyond which it was unsafe to venture. Her circle kept getting tighter.

She turned down the annual Girls Wild Night in New York. Each year at this time they spent a day and a night at the Pierre, meaning her Main Line chums Duffy and Buffy and Bootsie and Cutsie, and there, to escape husbands and children, they let loose, got drunk and high and always tried One New Thing.

I'd had broodings about the annual New Thing. This year's promised to be the best ever, according to Buffy. Joan gave her a flat negatory. I tried to persuade her to go and it was no use. She showed a strange side, wanting to know why I wanted her out of the house. Was I expecting someone?

She talked about building a hedge around our marriage.

"Enough with the hedges, circles and boundaries," I said. "Go. Air out."

To ignite her, I said, "What happened to this woman of the eighties I married?"

"She got older. Just like the eighties."

I began to spend my days in the library across from the shopping mall. I sat at a table overlooking an artificial lake and read the same books I had read as a child, about Babe Ruth, Lou Gehrig, Ty Cobb, Rogers Hornsby, Joe DiMaggio, Ted Williams. Sometimes, after a good fill of these books, I promenaded around the mall—the shops were always empty—accompanied by a roar of the crowd as I stepped up to the plate, seventh game World Series, bottom of the ninth, down three, bases loaded. *Drive deep to left . . .*

The roar of the crowd, as always, turned into the thunder of tanks racing across Sinai. Once or twice, in the past, I had tried to explain to her what it had all meant, and it came out so flat that the experience became diminished even for me. I realized that some things could not be told.

This day when I got back the house was dim and I heard Nat King Cole on the stereo. She had lit candles and incense and was curled up on the couch in a pink negligee, strawberry nipples peeking through the scrim. Her right hand was dangling between her thighs, a remembrance of kinkiness past.

"What's this?" I said.

"A seduction, you big lug."

"Aha."

"Interested?"

"Any special reason?"

"Women do have sexuality," she said.

"That's good news," I said.

"There has to be a reason? I'm horny. All right?"

"You know I don't like horny."

"I need you. All right?"

"That's a new one."

"Let's pretend we're not married. Remember how it was? The things we used to do?"

"I forgot."

"No you didn't."

"You think sex will bring it back?"

She dropped the baby talk. "Well, sex is what did this."

I turned on the lights and blew out the candles. "Sex and everything else."

"Josh, we have to get it back."

"I know."

"Otherwise—otherwise it's a terrible defeat."

"I agree."

"I mean, it means there's nothing."

"I've been feeling that way."

She said, "You've been feeling there's nothing."

"Right. Nothing."

"That's nice. Not that I haven't noticed. It's obvious you hate me."

"I don't hate you. I feel nothing."

"Oh that's very nice."

I said, "How can you feel anything?"

"Maybe I don't. But I'm trying. I'm trying."

"Believe it or not, I'm also trying," I said.

Her voice exploded in a gust of fury. *"Start loving me again god damn it!"*

"I never stopped."

"That's why you won't come near me? You haven't touched me since . . ."

"Yeah, since."

"Well I'm not contaminated."

"No, you're not contaminated."

"I'm the same."

I didn't answer.

"I'm the same. Joshua, I'm the same. Honest, I'm the same!"

CHAPTER
25

I FOUND the solution. Sleep. I went on a rampage. I slept everywhere. In shopping malls, on barber chairs, in restaurants, movie theaters, trains, at the kitchen table, on the couch, sitting, even standing. A strange promiscuity. I could do it anytime, anywhere, in any position.

What made me so tired was the knowledge that I had everything, a million dollars and the world's most glorious blonde shiksa for a wife. There is nothing more to have, I thought. This is it! The American jackpot! Bingo!

"See a doctor," Joan said.

"I'm not sick."

"Do you know how many hours you sleep a day?"

"I'm catching up. Had a rough childhood."

"You're not funny."

No, I was not funny.

In one sense I was better off than ever. The jealousy was gone. Used to be when I caught a guy giving her the eye I'd steam. Now, nothing. Anyhow, the risk of her being unfaithful was nil. In that respect she was thoroughly cured. She was even depleted of the urge to have fun.

This was not altogether terrific, the fun urge being the characteristic that had made her so triumphantly and endearingly American. Fun, after all, was America's religion. Remove the *fun* and we're no different from the Russians. (Talk to a Russian about *fun*.)

So this was finished. She even gave up tennis.

"I know what you're thinking," she said.

"Oh?"

"You're thinking of going back to Israel."

"That had been part of our plans."

"No, you're thinking of going alone, back to the army."

"Fat chance they'd take me again."

"Oh they'd take you all right. You're thinking of getting yourself killed."

"Frankly, there are eight hundred places around the world where it's even easier to get yourself killed. You don't have to go to Israel. In fact you can stay right here. Try riding a subway. You can get just as lucky."

"Yes, but you want to go down a hero. I thought you already did the hero thing in sixty-seven?"

"The hero thing?"

"You know what I mean."

"You don't understand, do you?"

"I do understand."

"No you don't. You never did. You never will."

"Because I'm a shiksa?"

"That has nothing to do with anything."

"Because I'm a woman? Because I'm a broad? Because I'm a cunt? Come on. Come on. Let's have it out!"

"I have no idea what the hell you're talking about."

"You hate women. Why, you're no better than Ibrahim!"

"You had to mention that name?"

"You're all the same."

"There's a universe between me and that other guy."

"Not when it comes to women."

We began to taste this bread of affliction every day. Every single day we got into another ugly flare-up, and these began to make her physically ill. She lost weight. She learned migraines. Her hands vibrated. Spasms developed under her eye, over her lip.

People, I thought, do not die from lack of love. Only dogs do.

I tried to fake it but she was no dummy. She could separate pity from love.

Still, she was undaunted. She had made up her mind. She had *decided* we were going to be as before, when life between us had been pure and sweet and sensational. That was it! Nothing else. Nothing less.

Maybe I didn't love her anymore, but I began to respect the hell out of her. One thing really got me. I did buy a ticket to Israel and she tore it up. "You're staying *here*," she said. She pushed me into a chair. "Here!"

I should have been furious except that I wasn't. I liked it, in fact.

She insisted, one day, that I take her out on a date. I managed to get us box seats at Vet Stadium and there, under the big lights, I turned to her to say something trivial and found myself staring. Her looks were *gone*. This caught me by surprise, how vacant she was! Now, her most prominent feature—at this bad moment—was a mustache. I had noticed it in the past and it had been ever so slight, given her natural blonde hair, and even now there wasn't much to it—just enough, though, to be repulsive.

"What's the matter?" she said.

"Nothing."

We had the best seats in the park, down along the rail on the first base side. Foul balls whizzed above our heads inning after inning and she said she had always wanted to catch one. The other team's Andre Dawson obliged, except that it wasn't foul.

The ball skipped over the first base bag and zoomed in at us, low, ready to ricochet into the glove of Philadelphia's outfielder. Joan reached down and gobbled up the ball. A terrific catch, except that on account of it the runner was awarded second base. He may have been thrown out had the outfielder been given a chance. The umpire declared fan interference.

The crowd—some thirty-six thousand—went berserk. Joan flashed her smile and held up the ball as a trophy. She thought they were cheering her. I said, "Joan, they're booing." She said, "No they're not." I said, "Yes they are."

She caught on when hot dog wrappers and beer cans came showering down and all those wrathful faces were turned on us. The jeers grew louder and louder. This was an inflamed mob.

I feared a riot. The stands were throbbing. Men in tee-shirts shook their fists directly at Joan and bellowed, "Whore! Bitch!" From the sound of it the entire world was in an uproar.

A stadium guard rushed to our side. At this, the crowd erupted again.

"You're gone," he said.

"What?" said Joan.

He grabbed her arm.

"Don't grab her arm," I said.

"You too, mister. You're both gone. Compliments of the management."

"All right, but don't grab her arm."

"Just follow me," he said. "Just follow me."

As we got up, the crowd cheered.

"But people do this every day," said Joan as the guard escorted us to the tunnel.

"The ball was fair," I said.

"How was I to know it was fair?"

"Let's go," said the guard. "You're losers."

"All right," I said. "Just don't be grabbing my wife."

"You're losers," he said.

The crowd kept cheering as we neared the exit. It was a long walk.

"I didn't know the ball was fair," said Joan.

"Let's just get out of here alive," I said.

"Is this the grand old game of baseball?" she said.

In the car, on the ride home, she was quite giddy. "We're not losers," she said.

"That's right."

"They're losers," she said.

"That's right," I said. But it's amazing, I thought, how it happens to people. When the magic goes, it goes. As if you're allotted so much grace—and, until recently, Joan

had never known a moment without heaven's charm—
and once it's used up, boy does it go!

This lady who had always been everybody's Miss Con-
geniality had just been booed by thirty-six thousand
people.

But she was defiant.

She said, "They're a sixth place team, aren't they?"

"That's right."

"They've only lost eight straight."

"Nine, counting today, most probably."

"We didn't lose the game for them."

"Maybe not."

"We're winners, aren't we, Josh?"

"I think so."

I liked the fact that she was defending herself and not
giving in. This was the Joan of old. But I did not care for
the urgency in her voice, something approaching panic.
She was being altogether too smug, which usually meant
she was wide open.

She said, "We've never lost eight in a row."

"Nine."

"We're winners."

CHAPTER
26

THE BASEBALL THING became a topic for weeks. She spoke of it in terms of delight. She was so proud of herself. They should sign her up, she said. She could play the game better than those people on the field. Did you see, she said, how I caught that ball?

Yes, I said. Everybody saw.

Bare-handed catch, she said. They needed *gloves!*

Fair ball my eye, she said. That ball was foul. Those umpires were losers. Those Phillies were losers. Everybody was a loser. The whole rotten stinking world. Big deal. Why do people care about a lousy stinking game of baseball anyway? That wasn't real life. Why do people care about *anything?* It's all the same. Everything's the same. We all die in the end. Huh! Even MacArthur died. He didn't fade away.

The way they carried on, she said, you'd have thought she had done something really harmful.

"Whatever happened to perspective?" she asked.

At the same time she was going on about these things she was reading a book in secret that had something like this for a title . . . *How to Win Back Love.*

The book was full of sound advice, as was another book she'd been reading in the bathroom.

We used to joke about all the books that were published. Name anything, we agreed, and there was a book on the subject, even a biography of Julio Iglesias, tops on our list of unrequired reading until I saw a title in a Sansom Street window—*The History of Mouth Sounds.*

But this book she was reading in the bathroom was something else again—*How to End It When It's Over.*

I confronted her. "A book on suicide?"

"I'm allowed to read whatever I want. It's a free country."

I ripped the book page by page.

"I thought we don't believe in book burning," she said.

"This is not a book."

"I wasn't going to do anything."

"Then why read?"

"I like to read."

"This is reading?"

She said, "If I wanted to do something I would just do it and be done."

"Why even think about these things? I thought you were so pleased with yourself."

"I am." Then she said, "Did you see how those people booed me? Me!"

"It's over."

"I'm booing back."

"Stop it, Joan. I thought we were winners."

"I thought so, too."

"Well?"

"We're all losers, Josh. Don't you know that? Nobody wins."

It wasn't much of a thing, this blemish that blossomed on her face alongside her left nostril.

I insisted it was next to invisible, this pimple.

"Don't say pimple," she said. "I hate that word."

No wonder. She had never had a pimple, even in her teenage years. In her silken days she had never known this type of imperfection. These, to her mind, were omens.

She said, "I have no idea why I should be breaking out now."

"One pimple is not breaking out."

"Don't say *pimple!*"

She became quite busy about this pimple.

"I know you're staring at it," she said.

She thought the entire world was staring at it, and it was true that it got worse from day to day. Soon, I said, it would be ready to pop. "Disgusting," she said.

We tried another date. "Let's go to Antonio's," she said.

"It's very expensive."

"So?"

When we entered the place I understood why she had chosen this over another. The lights were low.

"You're staring at it again," she said.

"In a place like this you need Braille."

♠   267   ♠

"Stop staring at it, please!"

"At what?"

"Stop!"

"Your pimple?"

"Stop!"

We sat there, ordered and ate. I watched the couple in the other booth, a glum middle-aged man and wife, not a word between them, trained, from twenty years of marriage, in the subtle skills of apartness. I had seen such couples before and was thrilled to think that it would never be this way with us—and now it was. We were that couple.

Finally, she said, "You're going to leave me over this. Over a *pimple*."

"Don't be ridiculous."

"You don't find me attractive anymore. I saw how you looked at me at the ballpark."

"You saw nothing."

"We mustn't go to bright places anymore."

"Come on, Joan."

"Now this. A pimple. A fucking pimple."

"I never heard you use that word."

"Pimple or fuck?"

"This is not you, Joan."

"You're right. There is retribution. He gets even, this God of yours."

"You got religion?"

"I wouldn't quite call it that," she said.

She saw a doctor. He lanced the stupid thing and it was gone. But not in her mind. In her mind it was still there, mountainous. She spread ointments on that spot—on that spot where nothing was—and hid that side of her face by keeping to profiles. Most mornings, now, she was reluctant to rise from bed. She was afraid to leave the house lest she be seen.

I tried to reason and in time I knew it would not work. Something had happened.

She had persuaded herself that the world had come to an end.

I had once taught her the mysticism of balances. The world was divided equally between good and evil. Therefore, the single individual held absolute power. By going one way or the other, the individual could tip the earthly scales either way. We had tipped it the wrong way.

No, not by what we had done in Atlantic City, but by what we had done in Philadelphia. We had stopped loving. This she saw as universally destructive. We had destroyed not only ourselves, but the entire world.

CHAPTER
27

THEN SHE GOT UP one morning in a terrific mood. She was ecstatic.

"I know," she said. "I know just the thing. We'll go to New York, the Empire State Building, and meet all over again. Do everything the same. Oh God, it was so wonderful that first moment! Let's do it, Josh. Oh please don't be practical or negative anymore. Let's do it, Josh. Start all over again.

"What room was it, you know, where we had that stupid meeting? Oh I fell for you so hard. That feeling I had. We have to do it, Josh. The same room. Even the *same room*. What was the number of that room? What floor were we on?"

I said, "I don't remember. But we can find out."

"We'll say the same things, all right?"

"I'm not sure we can get the same corpies back," I said.

"You're funny," she said. "Did I ever tell you you're funny? Isn't this a good idea?"

"It's an idea."

"Then we'll ride to the top, of course, and ride through New York to the Algonquin. Remember that? Remember how you got me up to the room? I had no intentions— well, I was really fighting you. But the way you smoothed in. Oh you were smooth. You said, 'For this kind of money they should throw in a room.' Was that planned, Mr. Smoothie?"

"No, it just happened. That may be a problem if we try it again."

"There won't be problems. Not if we don't want there to be. Okay? Please."

"Okay."

"Remember what you said up there?"

"Up where?"

"On top. You said, 'I understand on a clear day you can see Camden, New Jersey.' That was so good, Josh. That was such a good line. How could everything have been so perfect? Everything was so perfect."

The radiance was back. Remarkable how she changed. She went out, got her hair done, bought clothes, teased and flirted.

"What did you get?" I said.

"Clothes, silly."

"Can't I see them?"

"Of course not, silly. They're for New York."

In fact, everything was for New York.

I had no trouble locating the room in the Empire State Building, and as proof that things were going right again, the room was available and I rented it for an hour two weeks ahead and these were wonderful days, leading up.

At first I had been a reluctant partner in this scheme. You can't go home again and all that, except that nobody said anything about the Empire State Building. Besides, who makes these rules? I resented people making rules. Joan now had me up there with her. You can't relive the past. Can't rekindle a love that has died. Those were also rules—and so what? Let them make their rules their way and we'll live our lives our way.

We agreed to keep contact between us to a minimum so that nothing might spoil New York.

There was to be no bad talk, no sarcasm, no complaints, even about the weather.

"You're not eating," I said.

"I'll be perfect by the time we get to New York."

She proudly counted off the ounces she was losing.

"Getting down to striptease weight," she said, beaming that smile.

Yes, I remembered the striptease that first day.

Her figure had never stopped being sensational and it brought back memories, memories that had died. Some of the old lust began to heat me up. I began to feel rushed about New York.

I remembered the new things we had done—that first day in and out of bed—and her saying, shyly but willingly, "Like this?"

Erotic daydreams about her began to occupy me. I

thought of even newer things we might do and her saying, "Like this?"

Joan's fantasies, those she'd admit to, were on the opening scene, there in that meeting room in the Empire State Building. How we sat at the table with the others and flirted by not flirting, except for the occasional glance. How she read my thoughts and covered her knees. How we just happened to be in the same spot during the coffee break. How she had opened it by saying, "I know what you're thinking," and then all the fun we had at the expense of the corpies.

These (maybe the sex, too, she coyly allowed) were her fantasies. All of this, she warned, we'd have to get right, though there'd be no rehearsing. No, it had to be spontaneous.

It had to be fun and romantic and easy and most of all, it had to be the *same*.

I thought to caution her that this could be very difficult, making things the same—but I thought better. Hadn't I already decided to hell with the rules? Maybe, damn it, things *can* be made the same.

I knew a guy in Natanya, after all, whose house had been struck by lightning twice.

I once hit back-to-back exactas at the racetrack with the same two numbers, nine-two.

Again, yes, we were gambling, only this time there was nothing to lose. There was great risk, however. If we failed in New York, if it didn't click, the loss would be final, perhaps in more ways than one. There was something of the morning-glory about her exuberance, this bustle and zeal, such frantic high spirits.

We both knew the risk and didn't talk about it since there was to be no bad talk.

When I considered the odds I also had to factor in the element of streaks. The good run—when everything came up aces and jacks—was always a possibility, especially for a streak player like me. We had had a very good streak, then a very bad streak, and now maybe it was time for the good again.

I liked that thinking and I liked everything about us those two weeks leading up to New York. There was one thing still to be done beforehand, and I knew it would have to be approached with surgical precision.

I said, "I'm going to Atlantic City to withdraw our money. Do you have any objections?"

"No," she said, and all discussion about this was over. We both understood that the money was never to be mentioned again.

CHAPTER
28

I GOT UP EARLY in the morning. She was still sleeping when I got in the car and drove off. Nausea and loathing accompanied me when I turned onto the Atlantic City Expressway. I felt no better when I pulled up to the driveway of the casino. I had them park my jalopy. Inside, crowds surged in all four directions.

I walked straight to the cage.

"I'm here to cash in a marker," I said.

I gave my name and three IDs.

The clerk's name was Doris Whittingham, a pleasant, matronly type. She punched information into the computer and then vanished. I waited. It never occurred to me something might go wrong.

As I waited I had a nightmare of a flashback . . . We have survived mountains and oceans and here we are. I don't know where we are but there's a huge American flag above where we sit, in the waiting room. My sister sits neatly, clutching her Shirley Temple doll. My father and mother have that depleted refugee look about them, even after some years in Montreal. Men and women—Americans!—stroll back and forth, so well dressed, so easy, so tall. We're so *short*, I keep thinking. We are waiting for *papers*. Years earlier, on the other side of the mountains and the oceans, it had been *papieren*. Now it is papers. So we sit and we wait, and we wait. People are opening doors and closing doors, walking into this office, out of that office. There is one man my parents are waiting for. Where is he? Why is he taking so long? What does it mean?

What does it mean?

Finally he comes strolling toward us. My mother reaches for my father's hand. He does not notice. He's too busy watching the man come closer and closer. He keeps coming but it seems he will never arrive. He is not smiling. What does it mean?

"Mr. Kane?" he says.

My father rises.

"We'll be glad to give you a permanent visa," the man says, "except for one thing. Are you aware that your son has an irregular heartbeat? He didn't pass the physical."

My father knows enough English to understand the words—but he still does not understand.

"He's a healthy boy," my father says. His eyes begin to fill. "This boy," he says, "this boy walked up and down *mountains*! Isn't that healthy enough?"

"Has your son ever had scarlet fever?"

They confer in Yiddish, Mother and Father.

"No," says my father.

"Please wait," says the man.

Again he leaves and again we wait.

My mother says, "They won't let us in?"

Would even Canada take us back? By some error, Canada had already ripped up our citizenship papers.

"Shh," says my father.

"They won't let us in?"

"Shh."

"We have to go back?"

"Shh."

"Back where?"

Now here he comes again and he is smiling. He says, "It's probably just the excitement."

Then: "Welcome to the United States."

What does it mean? I asked myself when this Doris left me waiting.

Can't be, I thought. No, can't be.

What a dirty rotten trick. But it would serve me right, I thought, and then I thought—why? Why would it serve me right? What had I done? Plenty. Okay, that was fact. I had committed this and that transgression. But had I done anything so terribly wrong—in wanting a better life? Sy was correct there, wasn't he? This was everybody's soft spot. This was the *theme* of *every* life. Every living thing pursued this.

So what if it wasn't paradise when you caught this thing you pursued? This too was life.

I thought of the novelist James M. Cain. All of his books, he said, were about people whose dreams had come true.

♠   279   ♠

And all of his books were tragedies.

"Mr. Kane," Doris said. "This will require a joint signature."

"You mean the money is here."

"Oh yes. One million dollars, right?"

"That's right. One million dollars."

"It's here and ready to go, except that your wife has to sign for it, too."

"She's not here."

"Well, can she get here?"

"No. That's impossible. Never."

"I'll have to talk to my supervisor. I don't know what to do in a case like this. Is she sick?"

"Yes."

"Can it wait till she gets better?"

"No."

"The money will still be here."

"Listen, can't I sign for her?"

"It's against regulations."

"I'm her husband."

This was a wild complication. I knew Joan would never consent to coming down here, even for a million dollars.

Especially for a million dollars.

"She's very sick," I said.

"I understand."

"I'm afraid you don't. She's very very sick."

"Oh." Then she handed me the papers and said, "Sign these."

Forty minutes later she handed me a check.

"I hope everything is all right," she said.

"Yes. May I have an envelope for this?"

"Certainly."

I slipped the check into the envelope and tucked the envelope in my billfold and slid the billfold in the deep pocket on the right side of my jeans. I kept my right hand dug in as I marched out.

I waited for the car and when it came I heard a voice shout out my name.

But I knew all about turning back and I was gone.

When I got home Joan was on the couch reading the latest Bellow.

"Why do all his characters come off the page like alte cackers?" I said.

"Whose?"

"Below."

"Bellow," she said. "And I wasn't reading anyway."

"Oh."

"I was sitting here worrying."

"About what?"

"About you."

"I told you where I was going."

"I know."

"You sat here all day worrying?"

"Yes."

"Why?"

"I don't know. Something might happen."

"What might happen?"

"I don't know. Something."

"Like what?"

"They're shooting at each other on the highways."

"That's California," I said. "This is the rest of America."

"They're all over, these people."

"Well, nothing happened."

"I don't want anything to happen."

"You're afraid something might happen."

"I don't know. I don't know."

"You're afraid something might happen before New York."

"Maybe."

"Superstitious? My Joan?"

"It's not superstition. It's—maybe it's premonition."

"It's superstition."

"You think everything will be all right?"

"Of course. We're going to New York, aren't we?"

"Not soon enough."

"Ta da!" I said and I brought out the cane.

"Oh God, I forgot! How could I forget? The cane! Of course! The cane!"

CHAPTER
29

THE DAY BEFORE New York not a word passed between us. We had it planned that way, at least she had. We were to become strangers. Everything had to be coiled for the next day's explosion.

The meeting was set for eleven. There'd be just the two of us since, naturally, we were not about to hire a supporting cast of corpies. I had no idea how she was getting to New York—also planned. We were strangers, after all.

I assumed, however, she'd be taking the bus from Moorestown, so I decided on the train.

When I got up at six she was already in the basement between washer and dryer. I showered and dressed hurriedly and sped out. I caught the bus to Holmesburg and took the train to the Thirtieth Street Station and there I got on a Metroliner and in less than two hours was in the Empire State Building—to me, the symbol of America.

I unlocked the door with the pass key they had sent me and it was all there as before, the big table, thick leather chairs all around, and the memory flashed of her sitting there, that first time, so blonde, so beautiful. Suddenly, I wanted that back. I had not been a big supporter of this plan, but now I was, for any minute now she'd be walking in, and we'd have it all back.

Only we had it turned around. *She* was supposed to be here first. *I* made the entrance.

But it was only a few minutes past eleven, too early to be late.

I stepped outside and paced the hallway and eyed the elevators. Just as earth consisted mostly of ocean, so life, I realized, consisted mostly of waiting. Only two or three times in life was anything realized. The rest was waiting.

Then I walked back in the room and listened for footsteps.

Funny how it is when you're waiting. Every emotion takes a turn.

I wondered, did she remember the floor, the room? Did she remember the *building?* Did she have the right day? I picked up the phone and called her at home and there was no answer.

Elation. She left the house. She's on her way. She'll be here any minute. Bus must have got caught in traffic.

Weren't they doing work on the turnpike?

So the bus was late and she's in a cab right now on her way over, probably paying the fare right now.

I checked my watch—11:25.

The cab, I figured, was probably stuck in traffic. *New York.*

My God! I thought. New York! She could be anywhere.

Where do you start searching for someone in New York! You don't. You sit. Like this. Like this. Relax. She'll be here. She's got to be here. There is no other place for her to be.

But this room was starting to get very empty. That was all I could think of now, the hollowness of things.

Not for nothing, I thought, did it say, "A man without a woman is half a man." We were, all of us, Adam and Eve. Hermaphrodites. We split at birth, man and woman, and then went out searching for the other half of ourselves. Sometimes—rarely—we were lucky to find that other half. The tragedy was to find it and not recognize it, and this we called yearning.

Surely, I thought, she did not go out and do something stupid to herself. No, not when we were this close. Not when we had everything so arranged for the perfect comeback. This was supposed to be the beginning, not the end.

I remembered what she had said the other day. She had been worried something might happen. That had never been like her. Now—yes, since Atlantic City—she had become so afraid of things. She saw signs and portents. All of a sudden she believed in revenge bugs, those creatures that fly overhead and laugh at your dreams.

Now I heard footsteps, but too many. An army of corpies marched to the door.

"We're scheduled in here for noon," said the head corpie.

"It's all yours," I said, since it was noon.

* * *

She was in bed, the shades drawn.

"Hi," I said.

Her lifeless eyes were aimed an inch above my head.

"Hi," she said.

"You've been here all day?"

"Where should I be?" she said.

"Maybe New York."

"Oh."

"I was there," I said.

"Good for you."

"Did I do something wrong?"

"Not at all," she said. "You're a very good boy."

"Did you do something wrong?"

"Me? I'm an angel."

"Why weren't you in New York?"

"Me?"

"Joan. Come on."

"Come on, what?"

"Why weren't you there?"

"Because I was here," she said.

"I see."

"Yes, you see."

"No I don't see."

"I'm here."

"I know. But why?"

"Oh Josh, what's the use? It's no use."

"You were so excited about this."

"Was I?"

"Weren't you?"

"I guess," she said.

♠   286   ♠

INDECENT PROPOSAL

"What happened?"

"I got up this morning. That's what happened."

"You got up."

"That's what happened," she said. "It's a very bad thing to happen."

"Getting up."

"It's the worst thing that can happen."

"Getting up."

"Yes," she said. "It's a terrible way to start the day."

"I wish you had told me you weren't going."

"I didn't know I wasn't going."

"What made you decide?"

"This!"

"What?"

"This."

"What?"

"The pimple! The pimple! The pimple!"

I sat down on the bed. She turned her face away.

"I don't see a pimple, Joan. There is no pimple."

"Well then you're blind. It's as big as Mount Everest. It's ugly. Everything is ugly."

"Everything?"

"When you're ugly, everything is ugly."

"You're not ugly, Joan."

"You're very kind. I'm never leaving this house."

"Suppose there's a fire?"

"I tried to cover it up," she said, beginning to sob. "But it was no good. It's no good, Josh."

She ran to the bathroom. She was staying in there too long and I called out to her and she did not respond. I

♠   287   ♠

knocked on the door. Then I kicked it open. She was on the toilet seat cover, hunched over. In her hands were facial cream containers. Her face was smudged yellow and orange, especially that place near her nose.

I sat down across from her on the bathtub edge and took her hands and removed the bottles. Her hands were ice cold. I rubbed them and she sobbed in heavy spasms. She pulled me down so that I was on my knees and buried my head in her lap and now, frantically, she stroked my hair. "What happens to people?" she said. "What happens to people?" I tried to keep from sobbing and did not know whose tears these were running hot and fast down my cheeks.

CHAPTER 30

SO THEN in Haifa only now and then did I think of her, there in warships that went down to the sea to do business in great waters. I had joined the Israeli Navy as a volunteer, immediately after the separation papers made my split with Joan almost final, and it was not like joining the French Foreign Legion to forget. Or maybe it was.

I patrolled the Mediterranean on the Satile, warships America had used in Vietnam, and went into combat on the Zodiacs, inflatable rubber speedboats. In Hebrew there was no word for navy, so they called it Army of the Sea, and I patrolled the Mediterranean with this army of eighteen-year-olds, not counting officers of all ages. Once again I was in the Zahal uniform saying to my father, "Look at me."

Strange, though, because for the Israelis the army or navy was duty, no place to find oneself or lose oneself. Rather it was a chore, an unromantic task that robbed from the young the three best years of their lives. Glory— that was for the Americans.

But as for this American—I did not think about her anymore. It was finished. At the outset, yes, she had been on my mind. In bed in my bunk, so near the sea that I could hear the waves and through my windows see across to Acre and Lebanon, I wrote her imaginary letters. There was so much to tell. When mail came—though I had not told her where I was—I fantasized letters from her. But that was in the beginning. No more.

Anyway, it had been fifteen months since we decided it was finished. And no wonder. She had begun to waste away. Never mind love, the very spark of life had begun to leave her soul. She suffered terrible fits of depression, manifested by those migraines and sleeplessness by night, and by day she walked about hard and cold and she even jumped that time I tried to touch her. Words could not console her and she believed nothing she heard or read. She—Joan!—had turned cynical and even vindictive. The words "I love you" made her nauseous. Romantic couples—she scorned them. Most books and movies were about people in love, so she had nothing to read or see.

She still had the flair for the perfectly timed phrase— but now inverted. She said, "There will never be another you. Especially you."

She became a contradiction of herself. She was in the Norwegian night. Music and television were out and she even covered the mirrors, and our house was as a house of mourning. She spent all her days at home and hours in the bathroom, and there she tried to slit her wrists. Once. That was when we decided . . .

As for me, I had lost all affection for her. I had just been hanging in. Nothing of her was mine anymore. Even if she had been the same . . . but how could she have been the same?

No, it had been useless and terrible. Though I *had* tried, once even teasing and joking as in other days, just to reawaken even for an instant the old Joan—just for a glimpse. But there was nothing. Nothing left. Gone. All gone.

So here in northern Israel, in Haifa, beautiful and serene with a view of Mount Carmel from almost every point, the golden Bahai dome glistening against the sun, and even in view of Elijah's cave where nearby he contested the 450 false prophets of Baal and the 400 false prophets of Asherah—here I lived on the military base.

This base was bounded by the Mediterranean on one side and Aliya Street on the other. My schedule was a rotation of a week on patrol and a week of liberty, and in my free time there was so much to see, so many old friends to visit, and I did none of that, just stood outside the base, across the street, and watched the children play in the schoolyard.

This was Israel, this schoolyard. The old men and women, Israelis by way of Auschwitz, they also watched these children, so rambunctious and carefree, the trill of their voices a song to the martyrs even in their graves.

I wished she were here, too, to witness this, this incredible sight. First take her to Yad Vashem, there to see those pictures of those kids being shoveled from the ovens, and then bring her here to this schoolyard. Then she'd understand all the things I could never explain.

I remembered her saying that even if we had the most terrible fight and even if we split up, to always tell her where I was. She'd come find me. But who had expected anything like this?

I did seek her among the watchers, making a quick scan of the people outside the schoolyard. And she'd be easy to spot since there were no blondes within the entire land of Israel. No blondes meant no Joan.

But that was in the beginning and I did not think about her anymore.

We went out to sea that night in eighteen Zodiacs and then, on the shores of Lebanon, we silently deflated them and buried them and went in to avenge the slaughter of eight Jerusalem nursery students who had been taken to the bushes and slaughtered one by one by Arab soldiers and fighters.

In the exchange of machine-gun fire I got it again, same knee, but I held together until it was over and even helped dig up and inflate the boats and only later, deep in the Mediterranean, did I know pain.

They rushed me to Rambam Hospital and I was in there longer than I should have been, the doctor saying this knee, though it would heal, was telling me something. Longer than I should have been because, the doctor suspected, I had no will to live, which was not true. "You came here to die?" said Dr. Avri Ben Tov. "Come here to live!"

There was something strange about these Israelis. They resented heroes, even martyrs. They built monuments to them and sang songs about them and even wove legends around them but they resented them, maybe because their heritage and culture was dedicated to life, not death, and maybe because they had enough heroes, enough martyrs, and it was time for something else.

On this very base men who had singlehandedly defeated scores of Egyptians in Sinai and Syrians on Golan—they walked about unrecognized, meriting not even the basics, like a salute, though it was true that here nobody saluted and there was no clicking of heels.

In five weeks I was out of the hospital and back on the base, lame for the time being and out of commission, sinking deeper in my cot, and later sitting atop a rock, letting the sea flow beneath by feet, the sun gently warming my flesh.

In time, aided by a cane, I could walk for longer distances, even to the outskirts of the base, at last to Aliya Street, to stand outside the schoolyard and watch the children play.

The blonde lady . . . from behind she could pass for Joan. I had not thought about her at all. Not at all. But blondes—going back to the States—so many of them looked like Joan from behind and then they made the mistake of turning around. Such disappointment.

For a time, after the separation, I had tried to reconstruct Joan, even create a Joan, my own Joan. Let us make Joan. Some of the blondes that evoked such fantasies were *nearly* Joan and I thought, this could be Joan . . . but needs work.

Now—now the percentages were remarkably good. Here in Israel. A blonde.

A gambling man would bet that this was Joan.

Such a rare thing, a blonde, here, that I had to move closer, but not too close. Not yet. Let it last, the possibility. As long as her back was to me I could hope. No need to rush in and shatter this. This was delicate. I imagined her turning around and finally . . . finally Joan. That smile.

How close, I thought, would this golden-haired lady be to Joan? How *nearly* Joan would she be? Straight flush? Royal flush? *Jackpot!* I remembered, now—of all the memories!—that time more than a year ago in Atlantic City at Showboat, her getting that royal flush and winning almost nothing because she had used only a quarter . . . and how delighted she was! Thrilled and ecstatic and nary a thought to the minus, only the plus. Before that, on the tram, waving to the people on the Boardwalk, turning your basic tram ride into a magical adventure.

In the *cheder ha'ochel*, the mess hall, there had been talk of a blonde one. Couple of cadets had spotted this phenomenon. Scouts had even been sent out to spy. I had failed to make the connection, or maybe just thought it too incredible.

It had been so *final*.

So she had been here for some days, this blonde lady standing outside the gates of the schoolyard, and now I watched her and everything about her was a perfect Joan—at least from behind. There remained only this: for her to turn around.

Just like her—if in fact this was Joan—to know that this would be my pastime, watching these children. Of course she could have simply walked up to the sentry and asked for me, so maybe it wasn't her.

Two boys in the schoolyard were now in a tumble. Light sparring had flared into a mean fight and it was obvious there was a long-standing grudge between these two.

The big one had the smaller one on the ground, had him smothered and pinned solid. Not a happy sight, observing the smaller kid raging and flailing helplessly.

Come on kid. Push your two thumbs together and press up against his nostrils.

This is Krav Maga country. You should know this!

The blonde lady, now she turned, faced me and said, "Do something!"

I rushed in and broke it up between these two. Then I walked out of the schoolyard and stepped up to the lady. She was smiling, but her lower lip was quivering. I was quivering all over.

Crazy, I thought. No fear for even the most vicious hand-to-hand combat. Up walks this blonde and you turn to jelly.

But then, she was incredibly beautiful. I had seen something like her only once.

She said, "Not bad for a guy with a cane."

"Yeah, I had some trouble."

"Out at sea?"

"Yes."

"Still you on one side, the world on the other?" Her eyes turned red and began to swell. "Isn't that right?"

I hated to tell her that so far it was no contest. The world was way ahead.

I said, "I hate to see the bad guys win."

"I know just what you mean. So you have to keep on fighting. Especially for something very rare and precious."

"Yeah," I said. "You have to keep on fighting."

"Yes we do," she said. "I guess that's why I'm here, Josh."

SIGNET

Published or forthcoming

THE RATING GAME

Dave Cash

Behind the glass-fronted walls of CRFM's 24-hours-a-day nerve centre in the heart of London, three people fight for control of their lives as the tycoon powerbrokers of international finance move in for the kill . . .

Monica Hammond, the radio station's beautiful and ruthless Managing Director – nothing was allowed to stand in her way . . . until one man discovered her fatal weakness.

Nigel Beresford-Clarke – CRFM's greatest asset – hopelessly betrayed by his love for a schoolgirl . . .

And **Maggie Lomax**, uncompromising and tough as nails – then her outspoken broadcasts pushed the wrong people too far . . .

They're ready to play . . . *The Rating Game*

SIGNET

38 NORTH YANKEE

Ed Ruggero

When an unarmed convoy of American troops on a training exercise is ambushed by North Koreans near Hongch'on, the fragile peace that has existed since 1953 is shattered, and once again the US Army is in the front line of a war on foreign territory.

38 North Yankee is the blistering story of the men and machines on both sides as the powder-keg of Korea explodes into a bloody and ruthless struggle for military supremacy.